ALSO BY SUSAN THAMES

*As Much As I Know*

# I'LL BE
# HOME
# LATE
# TONIGHT

# I'LL BE HOME LATE TONIGHT

*Susan Thames*

VILLARD

NEW YORK

VILLARD BOOKS is a registered trademark of Random House, Inc.

Library of Congress Cataloging-in-Publication Data
Thames, Susan.
I'll be home late tonight / Susan Thames.
p. cm.
ISBN 0-679-41916-0
I. Title.
PS3570.H3184M34   1997
813'.54—dc21   96-49847

Random House website address: http://www.randomhouse.com/
Printed in the United States of America on acid-free paper
24689753
First Edition
Book design by Victoria Wong

*For Florence Fox Thames*
*and*
*Joy Anita Tomchin*

*and in memory of*
*Bobby Goldberg Fox*
*and*
*Etta Getzoff Tomchin*

*with love*

# _Acknowledgments

This book is not the book I set out to write, but I am not the writer who began it. Both the book and I are different, and I hope better, because of the early and patient readings of my agent, Joe Spieler; the pithy and pointed guidance of my editor, David Rosenthal; the tireless and inspired companionship of ongoing readers Laban Hill and Elise Whittimore Hill; the steady faith of readers Darren Henault and Julie Erikson; the clear intelligence of Robert Olmstead, Laura Kalpakian, Maggie Brown, and John Hoffman; the careful and loving eleventh-hour readings of Suzanne Gardinier and Melvin Jules Bukiet; the joyful audience of Toinette Lippe; the sage blue pencil of editor Ruth Fecych and the meticulous brown pencil of copy editor Jean-Isabel McNutt. Also of valuable assistance were the maps of Charles Neuschafer and his New World Maps, and fellowships from the Virginia Center for the Creative Arts, Hawthornden Castle International Retreat for Writers, and Yaddo, Inc. Finally, though neither last nor first but always, this book is done and I am not only better but well in large part because of the remarkable friendship of Joy Tomchin.

# I'LL BE
# HOME
# LATE
# TONIGHT

# Chapter 1

It was 1957, I was twelve years old, me and my mother June were gassing up the Buick at a filling station in Welch, West Virginia, on our way to the rest of our lives. Welch was where we'd been for the few months since we'd run off from home—Covington, Virginia, white paint peeling from the clapboard, pigeons nesting in the garage roof, people there who loved you so well and did you so wrong it made you feel like damning them all to hell, my grandmother off, my father gone, my mother sitting right there in that car beside me and for God knew how many years to come, somehow the best and the worst of the lot, close as skin, distant as memory.

Six months with June's cousin Sally and her husband Neil, six months of snit and nerves and bad cooking so I had an itch to go, but I had an itch to stay too, like you do when it isn't so much leaving as it is leaving for you-don't-know-what that cuts you in two. On the subject of leaving, June was undivided, but even if she hadn't been, Sally showing us the door made it a very simple matter.

Of course my mother, damned or not, was a very forward-thinking person. "Fate and gumption have made us a pretty pair of travelers, Lily," she said, and she winked at me as she took a piece of Clove chewing gum from its wrapper. "But never forget," she added, "a traveling woman with a strong sense of direction has nothing to fear." She folded the gum neatly into thirds, put it on her tongue and breathed hard, and I could smell the spice and the sugar. I helped myself to a piece—it smelled better than it tasted—and listened to the gasoline meter click off the tenths of gallons and the dollars and cents.

"Do you know the difference between north, south, east, and west?" June asked.

I turned the gum over in my mouth and wondered if this was one of her trick questions. "The sun rises in the east and sets in the west," I answered, because, after all, what could she make of that?

She yanked at the cuff of her white blouse and puffed up her fine yellow hair to give it some heft and height. "That's right," she said, still fussing with her hair. "So if it's the first thing in the morning and you're lying flat out on the ground with the sun to your left, then that's the east, to the right is the west, the south is at your feet, and the north is atop your head." She turned the key in the ignition, smiled too hard at the pump boy, thanked him for doing such a fine job cleaning the windshield, and pulled out of the station.

As we rode out of Welch, I knew I was seeing the place for the last time—the churches and houses, a park, the department store, the five-and-dime—and I wanted to ask June if we could stop, if we could stay just long enough for me to get out of the car and touch the gate in front of the library and smell the steam seeping out the open window of the coffee shop across the street, but I didn't say a word because I didn't like to let on to her that I cared. And then, as if she knew, she put her foot on the gas and sped past the sign that marked the limits of the town.

We were already crossing the Clinch River when she adjusted the rearview mirror, checked her lipstick, and pointed to the map of the eastern United States open on the seat between us. "Listen to me," she said. "When you're reading a map, the east is always on your right, the west is always on your left, and so on and so forth. The weather's going to start cooling off pretty soon, so we're heading south. All you have to do is keep track of the towns we pass through. Find West Virginia, and then find Welch over near Kentucky. In Welch, look for a road marked with the number sixteen, and then just follow it. That way, you'll always know where we've been and where we're going."

"Where *are* we going?"

"What's the next town south of here?"

I set the map in my lap. It took me a while to get my bearings on paper. Route 16 was a skinny pink line that ran north to Mullins or south to Tazewell. "Tazewell."

"Can we get there from here?"

"Sure thing."

"And then?"

"And then . . ." I traced south with my finger. "Marion and then Jefferson and then Blowing Rock and then . . ."

"All of those places are south of here?"

"Uh-huh."

"Good."

The sky was clear and the air was sweet and dry and the wind talked to my face through the open window. Smoke rose in twisted spirals from fires set at the edges of fields, and children stared and waved from school yards and fence posts and porches. All that day I watched the hills swell and spill into the hollows and let the first fall colors make me happy and sad for their beauty and what they signified: nature's wonders, the end of summer, me and my mother adrift.

June said we'd aim to average two hundred miles a day. She said we could do more, but she didn't feel like pushing herself. She also said that if she drove too fast, she wouldn't be able to look at the scenery, and since that was part of why we were taking this trip she didn't want to cheat herself. On the other hand, the money saved from her afternoons doing the bookkeeping and measuring yard goods at the fabric store in Welch wouldn't go but so far, and the last thing she wanted was to end up broke in some dinky little motel in Georgia, which was exactly where, just that morning, Sally'd said she'd expect to find us if she ever came looking. I said two hundred miles a day sounded like a good distance, but the truth was it didn't mean much to me. I suspected that distance was a lie, same as nearness—what was close often seemed so far away and what you'd left behind or what had left you haunted you still.

Now, for the first time since I was born, June and me were alone together day and night. We got it down to a routine, planning our route over breakfast, staying at the cheapest motel with a TV—though we hardly ever watched the shows because we were too tired or else because we weren't tired at all, and who wanted to sit on a lumpy bed and watch television when we could be chatting with the other travelers in the recreation room or the office or going for a stroll to see the town?

Taking evening walks worked best to ease us out of whatever we'd troubled each other over during the day. Usually it was something about the past, about Covington, something so silly you'd have to wonder why either of us bothered with it—the color of a neighbor's new patio furniture, whether we went to the Baptist or the Methodist church last year at Christmas. But every now and then one of us said something meant to cause the other pain, or test her loyalties—whether my grandmother Caroline lied about her age, was my father Nate's old Pontiac a two-door or a four-door?, and was the upholstery leather or cloth? It seemed like just the mention of their names was all it took for one of us to slam a hand against the seat or the car door or throw something, an empty Coke bottle, a dirty sock, or jump up and down in a fit. And once it began, we could keep at it for a long while, until one swipe at the air too close to somebody's chin or one word more malicious than the rest silenced me or her and the other was sure to follow, as we retreated to the far sides of the car seat.

On her side, June pinched her cigarette tight between her lips, one hand on the wheel and the fingernails of her other hand chipping away at the cuticle and red polish of her thumbnail, her face steeled beyond knowing, though I did study her, reading her with the eyes and ears of my skin trying to sense if I'd gone too far. But if in my mind I practiced the things I could say to make it up between us, I never did speak them, because it vexed me so that I feared her whim or her judgment. Just the same, I worried myself into such a sweat I could feel it trickle from under my arms, and I grew so lost to real things seen or spoken that the sound of her voice startled me when she said, "Dig around in my pocketbook and find me a pack of cigarettes," or "You want to stop soon or you want to drive a while? Perry Como's on tonight." I'd find her cigarettes and we'd pull in at the next tourist court early enough to have our walk, eat some scrambled eggs or share a pot-roast dinner in a coffee shop, and get back to our room in time to join right in with Perry, "Dream along with me, I'm on my way to the stars."

On our first day out of Welch we came to a number of agreements: We'd take local roads, so we wouldn't wake up some place a hundred miles away and not know the land we'd passed through; we'd stop anyplace either of us wanted to, whether it was for a look or a drink of water or just to stretch our legs; and we wouldn't pick up hitchhikers, since with all our clothes and the collection of remnants June had saved from her job—white linen, white velvet, white corduroy—the trunk was full and there wasn't even room for a rider in the backseat.

Those agreements worked pretty good until we made a couple of wrong turns. When she saw we'd entered Alabama June said it was the most miserable day of her life. She admitted that she herself was touchy on the subject of race, but touchy was one thing, bigotry was another, and there was more bigots in Alabama than there was fools in love.

"There's bigots in Virginia," I said. "What makes Alabama worse?"

"In Virginia we hate colored," she replied very matter-of-factly. "In Alabama they kill them."

I didn't hate them, but this didn't seem like the right time to mention it. "We could turn around and go back the way we've come," I said instead.

June said that, against her better judgment, she'd turned back the way she'd come once before, but she'd never do it again. Then just outside of Gadsden, she hit the brakes and told me to roll down the window. A sandy-haired man with a cowboy hat in his hands spit in the dirt, leaned into the car, and smiled. "Where you headed?"

"We're headed south," June said. It was only three words, but she stretched them out so they gave her the time she needed to size him up. And I guess he was of good measure, because when he said south was the only way to go, June told me to push over.

His body was hot and his strong smell—lemony and earthy at the same time—made my head spin and my stomach roil. He talked on and on like he'd been alone for too long and at first, I thought maybe I could be some consolation to him, but it always seemed like June beat me to it, with her animal eyes gone soft and her long polished nails flashy and red when she ran her fingers through her hair, and after everything he said, she said, "Gosh" or "Great sakes" or "You don't say," like consolation was all she knew.

His name was Willis, he was a driver for a bus company in Jackson—and wasn't that a sad state of affairs, he said, bus driver with no vehicle of his own. He'd been married five times with not a single child to show for it, he spoke Korean and a little Japanese, and he was on his way to De Kalb to bury his brother. June spoke her regrets and he said thank you and when she asked him where De Kalb was he said for her not to worry, he'd tell her what turns to make.

We stopped at dusk to get something to eat at a diner that had a German shepherd tied up to the trunk of a white pine near the door to the kitchen. I let June and Willis go inside and I inched up toward the dog to pet him. He wasn't more than a puppy, but his fur was all matted with burrs and his eyes were runny with sores. I thought leaving him to tug and strain at the heavy chain and collar was about the meanest thing I'd ever seen. I was talking sweet talk to him and he was wagging his tail, his sick eyes shining at me. But when I reached my hand out to touch him, he bared his teeth and growled. It was the silliest thing, I knew, but that shamed me so. And I thought I ought to leave the filthy cur alone, but something kept me standing there and it came to me that I liked letting him have his say, so I egged him on, making wet-lipped kissy sounds and tossing handfuls of dust at him, watching spit bubbles pop around his pink gums and yellow teeth. When the back door opened and a colored man in a stained white shirt threw out a dish of slops to the dog, I lost his interest. The man smiled at me as he let the kitchen door slam shut and a thousand blackbirds flapped their wings and squalled from their roosts in a huge elm tree nearby. Then the birds settled down again and the air grew still.

Inside the diner I took a seat across from Willis and beside June at a corner table, in the direct line of a big fan. June was whipping her fingers to draw the cool air to as much of her chest as she could expose without making herself look altogether ridiculous, given that it wasn't even that hot a night.

Willis said to have whatever we wanted, because it was his pleasure to take us to dinner. June gave his hand a little squeeze and said, "Oh, Willis." We all ordered fried chicken and mashed potatoes. I meant not to like it, but the gravy was good and salty and the chicken was crisp as crackling and I ate every bit on my plate and some of what June left on hers.

All the while, her and Willis talked about the silverware, the placemats, the waitress's hair, the counterman's eyeglasses, and it was just like their talk in the car, it sounded simple but it wasn't, because neither one of them was saying what they were really talking about. I tried to get a word in every now and then, but it seemed useless, and when a man got up from a table nearby and left a newspaper folded on his chair, I wiped my greasy fingers on my napkin and grabbed what turned out to be only a few pages, mostly classified advertisements for jobs and houses for sale or rent. I liked one description of a bungalow on a lake with a bedroom view of the water and the hills on the other side and I wondered if $27 a month was a lot of money.

When we finished our meal, Willis told June he'd drive for a spell if she wanted, and June said that'd suit her fine. He asked if the trunk was full, because it would be a lot more comfortable if I could ride in the back. But she said there wasn't any room in the trunk, so they decided we wouldn't stop anywhere that night, just drive straight through to Willis's brother's house.

He put on the radio and June found a station playing Tony Bennett and Frank Sinatra hits. "Remember this one?" she said to me right at the beginning of "All the Way," and she sang a few words. "Come on, Lily, you know this song," she said, and she poked me in the ribs with her elbow and when I still wouldn't sing with her, she pushed me hard against the door. "I'd like to put you in the trunk," she said, just loud enough for me to hear.

I don't know how far we were from De Kalb, but it must have been a few hours' drive. I don't remember when I fell asleep or who carried me into the house and upstairs to the bedroom where I woke up in the morning. The curtains were drawn, but I could hear heavy rain pounding the roof. I found the bathroom down the long hall and peed and washed my face. On my way back to the room I'd slept in, I could hear June and Willis behind a closed door. Some of it was talk, which was how I could tell it was them, but some of it wasn't. All I knew about my mother made it no surprise to me that she was sharing a bedroom with a man who wasn't my father. I wasn't surprised, but I wasn't happy.

I got back under the covers and waited for someone to come for me and tell me what was next and I fell back to sleep, I guess, because when June came in with a cup of tea, she had to shake me hard before I came around.

"It's your favorite, orange pekoe," she said, setting the cup on the nightstand. "Did you sleep okay?"

"Are we going to stay here?"

"It *is* a pretty room, isn't it?" she said, and she circled the braided rug in a pair of somebody else's high-heeled shoes, looking at the chair slipcovered in a chintz to match the curtains and the dust ruffle on the bed.

"Where's Willis?"

June sat down beside me and sipped my tea and smoked the cigarette she'd dug from the pocket of her skirt. "He's seeing to his brother," she said. "He'll be back soon, probably only just in time to see us off."

I took the tea from her. It was still steaming hot, but I drank some of it because it was mine. "Where are we going?" I asked her, and she started to answer, something about passing through Pensacola and Tallahassee and winding up in Vero Beach, Florida, but to me those sounded like names on a map, not really answers at all, so I asked her again, "No, I mean where are we really going?"

June took the tea back and yapped, "What the hell are you talking about?"

"Give me my tea," I said.

"I'm drinking it," she said.

"Make yourself another cup and give me this one," I told her and my voice was loud, I could hear it, and I could see it loud on her face.

"Just who the hell do you think you're bossing around?" she said, and she made her eyes turn to mean slits and she brought the tea to her lips and sipped some and then she told me to go wash up while we still had the time.

I knew it was no accident when I got up from the bed and knocked the cup right out of her hand so the tea spilled on her lap and turned her blue skirt purple. She jumped up and hollered my name loud like it was a dirty word and held her skirt away from her, and when she looked at me there was pain and disbelief in her eyes and I was glad to see it. Her cigarette was still burning where it had fallen from her hand to the braided rug. I pointed to it. "Better not set the house on fire," I said and I turned and walked away.

In the bathroom, I stood in front of the medicine-cabinet mirror and wrote my name in what was left of the steam from June's shower. Then I turned on the water, stood under the needles of the hard spray for as long as I dared, sang "All the Way," hollered, cried, and when I heard the telephone ring downstairs, I pretended it was somebody calling from Covington to tell me to come home, Caroline, Nate, Nate, Nate, and I gave him hell for waiting so long and I beat the grout between the wet tiles till my knuckles bled.

When I got out of the shower, June was standing in the bedroom, waving her skirt to make it dry faster. She asked me did I know that carrying on like she'd heard me doing in the bathroom was what made me kin to Caroline. Then, as she turned to leave the room, she said it had been Willis on the telephone, he was going to be a while and we weren't going to wait to say good-bye. "So put some Band-Aids on your goddamned hands," she said, "and meet me at the car."

# Chapter 2

It was always like that between me and June, we had each other coming and going. When I was a little girl, she used to wake me in the middle of the night and together we'd sneak out of the house to ride the back roads in Nate's two-tone Chevrolet. I liked night riding, June so close beside me I could smell her sleepy skin, while I nodded to the perfect rhythm of the tires thudding on knotty pavement and stared into the pale funnels the headlights cast into the woods. On rainy nights I liked to click my teeth with the windshield wipers' clacking and follow the path of the water as it rose up the glass in snaky streams. On clear nights I liked to kneel beside the open window and stick my hand out to reach for the corn or wheat or wild grasses that grew right up to the edge of the road.

"You could slice yourself up doing like that, Lily," June once warned me, and then as if to prove herself right, she stepped down harder on the accelerator so the reeds and leaves of what grew well or wild in southwestern Virginia smacked and stung my fingers. "Doesn't it hurt?"

"Huh-uh."

"How come you're biting your lip?"

"I like it."

"You got your daddy's big lips."

"What do I have that's yours?"

June grabbed the wheel like she meant to pull it to her in an embrace. "You got my passion to keep moving," she said.

It was true, that *was* her passion, to be always going somewhere, so even when she was standing still you could feel her like she wasn't there, she was already on her way to the place she was thinking about or remembering, some big city or some swanky resort, wherever there was a lot of glamorous people and fine cars and restaurants. When she was still a little girl, her father had left them for just such places. Her mother's only regret was that he hadn't left sooner, he had a change purse for a heart and a shag rug for a soul. June's only regret was that her father hadn't taken her with him, to Nag's Head, the Breakers, Atlantic City, New York, Rehoboth Beach, but I suspect less exotic places would have done, anywhere but Covington, anywhere but my grandmother's house that June said smelled of overcooked meat and old shoes, no glamour there, only mirrors streaked with dust and Caroline's stifling ways—everything spare and lean except her love and her imagination, two things that, from all appearances, my mother doubted the value of.

To me, Caroline was a great bewilderment, maybe because she was more a child than I myself knew how to be, so I found her innocence and her faith both a wonder and a terror. As for Covington, I neither liked nor disliked it. My passion was for June, and if she was going somewhere, I wanted to go too, though it often happened that, by her side, I was unhappy, I was cross, I was as near and far away as love can make you as I was those nights riding in Nate's Bel-Aire.

Our first car was a Nash. I never remembered it except

from pictures, but it was the car Nate had when he met June. She was working at a cocktail lounge in Virginia Beach and it was the car they took on their honeymoon to Charleston. June said it was a small backseat for getting to know somebody and then two doors was a trial for a family with a child. So when Nate went on the road selling industrial-strength cleansers and deodorizers for the James Venery Victor Company and they offered him a company car, June went with him to pick one out.

It was a white four-door Pontiac with an all-white cloth interior and white sidewall tires, white to match June's wardrobe, which was white year-round, even though Caroline said it wasn't practical, to which June replied that a woman like herself, bound for bigger and better things than Caroline ever dreamed of, didn't have to trouble herself over such matters.

"To hell with practicalities," that's what June Prescott Wolsey said. "Give me style anytime." I guess she knew plenty about style, despite how she was shaped, long and lean, with the places where a woman is meant to show some fullness like points of forgetfulness on her body. But if her hips and her chest were not memorable, and if her features— wide-set eyes, flat nose, and a rosebud for a mouth—were oddly assembled, then she more than made up for it with the way she walked and the way she talked, which was neither one of them one way at all, but a thousand different ways, like she was styling herself over and over to suit the occasion.

My father, Nathaniel Wolsey, was also long and slim, and his features were as strange an assortment as June's—big ears and a nose of indecision, narrow and bony at the bridge and crooked as it made its way down to his full mouth, above which he sometimes wore a mustache of the same coal-black color as his hair. He had bottle-green eyes, heavy-lidded and thick-lashed like mine are today, and if I'm any example, every heart he won with those eyes was a heart he broke, his gaze went that deep.

The three of us lived with Caroline. It was always meant to be just for a while, because a while was all June could take under dreary Caroline's roof; it was always meant to be just a little while longer, until Nate got himself going, until he got up the capital to start something of his own, I thought capital was like Richmond, I thought a while was forever. Our home was the two-story frame house my grandmother owned, and they kept the car out back. Besides the Pontiac and a Ford, that two-tone Chevy is the one I remember best. It was new the year I turned nine, aqua and cream, with a chrome strip around the steering wheel that I liked for the sound I could hear if I was sitting right beside Nate. It was the tapping of his rings—wedding band, Masonic ring, pinkie ring—against the metal rim, as he made the turn into our driveway or struggled to back the big car into the garage that was built to hold a Model T.

June used to laugh at him where we stood in the backyard watching him park that big sedan. I remember one Friday in November of that year. She was humming some song soft and low, with her arms crossed over her chest and her red fingernails fanned out against the sleeve of her white wool blazer. "How is he ever going to make something of himself with the way he is? Why on earth does he have to do everything backwards?" she griped, as we watched him squeeze himself out of first the car and then the garage, with his valise in one arm and a bag of presents for us in the other. Why on earth did she have to go on at him? I wondered. But then I hummed that same song and crossed my arms across my chest and struck a pose to match hers.

June reached into her pocket for her cigarettes, lit a couple, one for her and one for him, and handed them both to me. "Hold these for a second, will you, Lily?" she said as he came up beside her, set the bag and the suitcase on the ground. Then they kissed hard and held each other so tight the heat seemed to rise off the two of them like the smoke rising from those lit cigarettes. "Missed you so bad," one of them said. "Me too," the other one answered.

But then the heat was gone, as if by agreement, and Nate let her go and grabbed me up, cigarettes and all. "You're too young to smoke," he said with his face right up close to mine the way I liked it. "Let me and your mama have those and tell me how you've been."

June took the cigarettes from me, passed one on to Nate, and dragged her feet as she walked ahead of us. "Put her down," she said over her shoulder to my father. "She's too big a girl to be carried around." I told him my news as I slid down against him till my feet touched the ground. Then he took the suitcase and I took the bag and we followed slowly behind my mother, with me dragging my feet—I wanted to be her, only better, and he let me think I was. "Missed you so bad," he said. "Me too," I answered.

Caroline was sitting at the kitchen table, listening to the transistor radio that hung from a black leather strap around her neck and polishing June's silver. She had her gray hair tucked up under a man's knit stocking cap, and she had on a big sack of a housedress to hide the swell of her stomach that had come when she went through her change. She was wearing the pair of old cotton gloves she used to clean the few odd pieces of plate and sterling June had picked up here and there, one glove for applying the pink polish, another for wiping away the milky film and the black tarnish—and she was smiling at her own reflection in the shiny face of a tea tray and singing the news back to the radio announcer and my mother's indifference when me and Nate let ourselves into the house.

"Hope you got something in that bag for me," Caroline said as we stepped inside. She drew me into her arms with a gloved hand. I could smell the black tarnish and then her breath heavy with tea and old age. I could feel real kindness on the outside and something like rapture underneath, and I was thankful for the one and fearful of the other.

"I got you a new switch for the attic fan," Nate said. He took the paper bag from me and emptied the packages onto the cracked yellow countertop.

"It's about time. And what did you bring for Lily?" Caroline said as she hugged me tight and then let go.

"Brought me soap and matchbooks," I said.

"And he brought me perfume," June said, scorn turning the edges of her tiny mouth to a pout.

"Windsong," Nate said.

"Cheap stuff," June said, "dime-store stuff, that's what you bring us, and then you want everything fancy when you get home. Well, you ought to know there's nothing fancy served in this house, so I wonder where you're eating supper tonight."

"I'm taking you all out," Nate said.

"You're not either," June said, which wasn't so much a statement of fact as it was an inside-out wish, saying the thing she didn't want, to hide the thing she did.

"Where's my soap?" I said, because I knew one way or another, I'd eat, but the four of us in one room was sometimes more than my appetite could bear.

Nate laughed as he took off his jacket and laid it over the back of a chair. Then he handed me a small brown paper bag sealed shut with a strip of Scotch tape.

"I got pork roast and boiled potatoes," Caroline said.

"I got a few telephone calls to make," Nate said.

"I got a headache," June said.

I kissed my father and ran with my present upstairs to my room. As soon as I opened the bag I was under the sweet-smelling spell of those little bars of soap wrapped in waxy paper—Camay, Ivory, and one bar I couldn't name because the print on the paper was a picture of a Quality Court in Danville. I added all but one of them to the collection I kept in a box under my bed, added the matchbooks to the other box, near to full, and lay back with a bar of Castile Delight, YOURS COURTESY OF THE HOTEL PATRICK HENRY, pressed to my face.

There was always at least one radio playing in our house, sometimes two or three, each tuned to the same station so we had stereophonic sound before they'd even invented it. Now I could hear my grandmother downstairs, singing along with "Shine On, Harvest Moon," and above her voice, the whistle of the teakettle, and then louder than either of those, the raised voices of Nate and June in their room across the hall.

"You bring me Windsong, but what's this other? Tigress, isn't this Tigress, Nate?" I heard June shouting through her nastiest laugh. Then she came stomping into my room with one of my father's shirts gripped in her hands, sniffing the collar, her face a mess of tears and anger. "Look at this, Lily," she said. "Collar's dirty as a dog but the shirt smells sweet as a plum cake." She handed me the shirt and pushed my face into the cloth and told me to smell it good, so I could make sure I knew what getting it smelled like on a man, and then I'd better make sure I was the one stinking up his clothes. Because if it was some other woman, I could be sure she was getting the rest—the nights out at the lake, the swell suppers, and the good champagne. My head was spinning from what she'd said and the way her words made me feel, frightened and cross like you do when you're caught in the middle of something but where you want to be is outside of it. Though to be more exact, where I wanted to be was outside of it *with Nate,* because siding with him was a way to get myself out of the range of June's great power, never mind that siding with him wasn't much of a side at all.

I think I stopped breathing when my father crossed my room in two big strides and tore his shirt from my hands. "Don't be that way, Junebug," he said, and there was real regret in his voice, I was sure. "You want to go out, I'll take you out. You get yourself fixed up, and we'll ride over to Gardner's. I'll call and tell them we're coming, ask them to hold the table by the window for us. They got a girl singer from Norfolk, I hear she's damned good."

"I don't care about any girl singer or Gardner's," June said. Her voice grew louder as she added, "And I'm staying right here tonight and having supper with Caroline and Lily. I came back to my mother's house just to please you. Well, you got what you wanted. I'm staying put. And I am not washing your shirts anymore. Do you hear me, Nathaniel? You can go naked for all I care."

"Jesus, Juney," he said as he broke a smile that let me breathe again, "I don't think they'll let us in if I don't put a shirt on, but if that's the way you want it, I'll give it a try. I might start something new." He winked at me and then he whispered to my mother, "I saw an advertisement in the Bluefield paper for a nudist colony in Myrtle Beach."

"What's a nudist colony?" I asked, glad as anything to have something to say.

"Go ahead," June said. "Tell her."

"It's a nature camp," Nate said.

"That's not what a nudist colony is," June said, and she turned to me. "A nudist colony is . . ."

Nate clamped his hand over her mouth and the two of them burst out laughing. Caroline called from the bottom of the stairs that supper was ready.

"We're going out, Mama," June called, "but Lily will be right down."

"Well, I'm ready to eat, so send her along," Caroline called back.

"I'm having a sirloin steak," June announced on her way out of my room, "and potatoes au gratin."

When we were alone, Nate told me that Gardner's had the best chocolate cake in all of Virginia and he said he'd bring me home a slice. But we both knew better. June wouldn't let chocolate in the house. She said it was bad for her skin, even the thought of it made her break out, and what was she paying good money to a fancy doctor for if she was going to ruin it all on some damned dessert?

Caroline said for me not to mind, and truth to tell I didn't, there was plenty of other good sweets my grandmother made, coconut custard pie and hazelnut cookies, and she always let me lick the spoon. On special occasions she made angel food cake. Once she told me there was things hidden in the wings of the angels and she stared at me hard with her blue-green-hazel eyes open wide. June said, "That's nonsense. You stop filling her head with such talk. And stop looking at her like that." But then she went off to White Sulphur Springs with Nate, and Caroline said we could go up to the attic, which was as close to heaven as we were allowed, and see what we could find hidden in our wings.

That time we found a diary written in a fancy hand, and all the entries were about a vacation trip to the Adirondack Mountains and a long train ride home. The diary was there among some musty books and brittle linens and an oval-framed picture of a naked woman stretched out on a sofa, all of it in a box right under the eaves. Another time we found a bag of marbles Caroline thought were her dead brother's. Did it make her sad to see them again? I asked her. She said it did and then it didn't, because hadn't we come up looking for angels?

I thought she was going too far with the angel business, but I didn't fuss when she started tearing through a dome-topped trunk looking for I didn't know what. I didn't know, that is, until she found it, an old dress, long and sheer, a summer dress with yards and yards of skirt that she dropped over my head and pulled down around me. "Hold it up by the hem," she said. "Hold it up so the skirt's your wings and then let me see you fly, my angel."

How could I get this over with was what I was thinking, so I gave the skirt a little shake and hoped it would satisfy her. "Not like that," she said. "You won't ever get off the ground if you don't do better than that. You got to pump hard, and stretch your neck out like this." She flapped her arms at her sides and pushed her chin out so her fleshy neck grew taut. Her eyes dropped shut, but even shut, they fluttered with her flapping arms. And I never meant for them to, but suddenly my eyes shut and my chin pushed out and my arms stiffened and flapped as fast as I could make them go.

"That's it," she cried, "Christ sake, that's it, I can feel it coming, I can feel us rising up, don't stop, honey, we are heavenbound."

I didn't stop, I couldn't, I thought maybe I was feeling it too, from the rush of air through my skirt and how I was standing on the tips of my toes and there was less and less holding me down. So I tried to pay it no mind when I heard Caroline running across the attic, but then I had to look when I heard her throw open the window, and there she was with one foot already through the sash.

"Caroline Taft Prescott, don't you fly out that window," I hollered as I raced across the room. When I grabbed her arm, her skin through the sleeve of her housedress was loose and cold and for just an instant I wasn't sure if I could save her, wasn't even sure I wanted to. But then, with the reach for my own levitation still so fresh and fiery in my recollection my skin covered with goose bumps, the sureness came, and I tightened my grip and pulled her toward me. She was stronger than me, of course, and still flapping her arms half in protest and half in flight. But she was precariously balanced there on that windowsill and soon landed in a flailing heap on the floor, singing my name too loud and reaching for me, sorry this, forgive her that, as I backed away.

"I don't believe in angels," I shouted with secret regret as I ran from the attic, tripping on the yards of that cursed skirt, the thrill and the horror of her ways burning me through and through.

Downstairs in my room, I tore off the dress and balled it up and threw it under a chair, which is where June found it the next morning when she came in to tell me about the Mountain Grove Hotel, the dancing and the music and the drinks they served with little paper flowers wired to the stems of the glasses. "What on earth is this?" she said, as she picked up the dress and held it in front of her so its yards of skirt billowed at her feet.

"Caroline's," is all I said.

"Caroline's what?" she asked.

"It's from the attic," I said, and I was getting ready to tell her the rest when she looked down to see where the hem finished a couple of inches above her ankles.

"Kind of pretty, isn't it? A little gaudy, I guess, but you never know. Some summer night. Once in a while I like a little color. With a few inches off the hem and a good dry cleaning. Fit you in a couple of years, that's one thing any-way." She folded the dress carefully and set it at the foot of my bed and lit a cigarette and looked at me. "You're sulking,

Lily," she said. "Damn, I hate it when you sulk. Looks nasty on you. Did Caroline have you up there in that attic torturing you last night? I told you to stay in your room when we go out. All she's good for is calling the fire department or the police. Damn it all to hell, I swore to God I'd never live under the same roof as that loony old woman and here we are, your daddy's promises nearly as useless as she is. Well, it won't last forever, and in the meantime you've got your books and games, and you can always take our radio. Next time, Lily, you do what I say."

*Next time, take me with you,* is what I was thinking. *We'll wear our dresses, white or flowered to match, and we'll dance with our partners, Nate and some other man looks just like him, it won't matter who. We'll dance without them. We'll dance and no one will rattle me with their magic if next time you take me with you.*

# Chapter 3

It turned out Willis's De Kalb was in Mississippi and a lot further west than June ever meant for us to go, so it took three days to get to Vero Beach. At the start my mother wasn't feeling good from her monthly, and we had to stop every couple of hours for her to use the rest room. She'd go in looking ashen, with a fine line of sweat above her top lip and her hair limp and straggling loose from the barrettes she used to keep it off her face. Then she'd come out looking like a new woman, a flush to her cheeks and her hair combed and neat, and even her clothes somehow free of the days of wrinkle and wear.

Most times we'd split a cold soda right there at the filling station or the store, sitting on a bench or a pair of milk crates, scratching our names or games of tictacktoe in the dirt, avoiding each other's eyes early that first day with the memory of hot tea and hot words still fresh on our minds, but then stealing a smile as the day wore on, and cracking jokes about the country boys who took our money for lunch—

sticks of beef jerky, bread-and-butter pickles, boiled peanuts, day-old kaiser rolls.

Back in the car, we rode in silence after June gave up on the radio—preaching, country music, static—and I watched a thousand worlds go by. Now where we were going didn't concern me so much, what there might be when we got there was the bigger question, and, unanswerable for all its immensity, it was a question I didn't ask.

After a while, June would stop once more to use a rest room, and I'd go too. Then she'd sit on the front fender and drink the first half of a Dr Pepper. I'd drink the second half standing beside her, then take the empty back inside, study the postcards, buy a piece of licorice, watch my reflection in the windows, moving my arms and making faces at myself to get a better idea of what I looked like. But I never believed what I saw. I had some other notion of myself that this image didn't match. I was taller and my hair was straight and blond, not thick and black, and my eyes were set far apart, not close and deep like the ones that stared back at me and then shifted outside to where June was leaning against the car door laughing with a boy in faded overalls about something that probably wasn't funny at all. Then we were driving again. The daylight faded. There was street lamps in the towns and headlights on the roads and the light from the dashboard pale on my mother's face.

At night, we stayed in guest houses because June said the one night with Willis had spoiled her, she liked getting things for free, and if they weren't free she wanted them cheap. These were dreary places, but they cost less than the motels and they gave you your meals for only fifty cents extra, although you had to eat whatever they were having and to my mind it didn't pay. After dinner, June went right up to our room and lay there not sleeping, which I knew because I could see her eyes open when I came up later. On the first night it was after I took a long walk and talked to somebody standing on a corner.

"Not much of a town, is it?" she said, as she sat up against the headboard and reached for the nail file she'd left on the nightstand.

"A man I met told me they got a feed store and a couple of churches and a doctor makes calls once a week."

"Like I said, not much of a town." She put down the nail file and asked me for her hairbrush and told me to sit there on the bed beside her. A good hour is what it took to get through all my knots and snarls and we hardly spoke a word except for what she said when she finished. "You got the most beautiful hair, Lily. You know your hair and your skin are your best features." I touched my hair, touched my cheek too, tried to love what she loved in me. Then she passed me the brush and told me to be gentle and I was, I know, because after just a minute or so, she slipped down on the bed and turned her back to me so she could let my strokes put her to sleep.

On the second night I borrowed a rusty old bicycle from the woman in Chattahoochee who fed us biscuits and gravy for supper and said there was more for breakfast and sent me down for a look at the river. Muddy river, sluggish, bats flying low among the branches of the trees that hung over the water, old boots and tires and a busted kitchen stool and a little colored boy in a pair of plaid shorts and a torn undershirt with a faded picture of Santa Claus and Rudolph on the front and "Merry Christmas" written on the back.

"I ain't afraid of bats," he said to me as I came up alongside of him.

"Me neither," I said.

"My mother's afraid of 'em. Had one fly right at her once when she was a girl. Starlings do the same thing sometimes when their young is feeding." He stirred the mud with a long stick. I searched the brush of the bank for a stick for myself, found one thick as a table leg, and joined him. "I'm seven," he said.

"I'm twelve," I said.

"You're big."

"So what?"

"I'm small. But I'm smart."

"I'm smart too."

He looked at me and then he looked at my stick. "Smart girl wouldn't bother with such a big stick. You can't hardly lift it."

"I don't want to lift it."

"Oh." He stirred the mud some more and raised the end out of the water. Something black and slick was hanging from the tip.

"What's that?" I asked.

"Nothing," he said and dropped the end back into the mud. "How late can you stay out?"

"Late as I want."

"Me too. I can stay out all night long if I want. That's what I'm gonna do, stay here all night."

"Won't they miss you at your house?"

"No."

We stirred the mud for a while. I felt something tug at my stick and I tried to lift it for a peek, but I couldn't. We listened to the bats' wings beat the air and the crickets sawing and the night birds telling their news. There was no moon and no stars and everywhere was dark and the river looked darker than the sky.

"What's your name?" I asked him when all that darkness bore down too hard for me to bear it in silence.

"Evander."

"What kind of name is that?"

"It's my name. What's your name?"

"Lily. It's a flower."

"I seen some, they was white, at Eastertime."

"There's other colors too, yellow and orange, daylilies are orange. Did you ever see them, how they turn their heads to follow the sun across the sky?" Evander looked at me like I was lying. "That's just what they do. They grow thick along our road back home. June used to say they were like a bunch of silly girls, all of them in a fit over the same man, and living just for the sight of him."

"Who's June?"

"My mother."

"My mother's name's Ethel but I call her Mama. I got a sister named Ella. We live on the other side of the river, over there where you can't see. We got chickens and a pig." Evander began to walk up and down the bank, pulling his stick behind him, tracing tracks in the mud, talking about his mother and Ella and the chickens and the pig like children do, so sure that you're listening. Which I was, not so much to the things he said as for the way he spoke, letting my ears blur the way I sometimes did with my eyes, so everything got fuzzy and his voice was like a song.

He was still going on, about an uncle I think, or a cousin named Lester, when I let my stick sink into the mud and trailed his route, walking in first one direction and then back the other way. The boy's snaky path tugged at my feet with each step. I heard new birdcalls now, maybe some kind of Florida bird, something beautiful and scarlet, and then a train whistle somewhere in the distance and Evander deep into another part of his story about his uncle or his cousin playing a game of golf with a white man for an acre of land, and how this Lester had figured out how many square feet of land he'd get for every hole he played and how many rows of corn and tomatoes he'd plant for each swing of the club.

Muddy banks and crazy birdcalls and swinging golf clubs tired me out, especially the golf clubs and the mud. Evander followed me as I wheeled the bicycle up the path and out into the street. From the top of the hill, all sight of the river was lost in the thickets and the night. I took a running jump onto the bicycle and as I began to pedal, I heard his footsteps keeping up with me. Then he was right there beside me and, just like we'd practiced it a dozen times before, I lifted my near hand from the handlebar and raised my arm and he grabbed hold of my far arm for balance and leaped onto the stretch of frame that made it a boy's bike. Riding sidesaddle, he curved himself to match me, his woolly hair right under my nose, and his smell was lye soap.

Our Buick was at the far end of the street, parked in front of the house with the hand-lettered sign hanging from a post at the top of a short flight of wooden stairs, HOBSON'S GUEST HOUSE, where me and June had the spare room on the second floor. The light was on in that second-floor room and June's silhouette still as a cutout at the window. I stopped the bicycle and Evander slipped down to the ground so quiet I had to give him a second look to see what he was made of. In the glow of a street lamp I could see him better now than I had down by the river. His big lips were smooth and his cheeks dimpled when he smiled at me and said good-bye.

By the time I got up to our room, the lamp beside the bed was turned off and June was lying on her back with the covers tucked under her arms and a cigarette burning in the ashtray. "Was that a little colored boy?" she asked.

"When?" Hers was a trick question, but so was mine.

"Just now, got off the bike you were riding. Looked colored to me."

"I don't know. I didn't ask him."

"Christ, Lily, you don't have to ask if somebody's colored.

That's the point." June took a long drag on her cigarette and held the smoke inside her for a while, and then she blew it out in a thin fine stream.

I went to bed in my underpants and nothing on top. The sheets were scratchy against my bare back and I tried to lie still so I wouldn't chafe myself. June put out her cigarette and turned over on her side, and pretty soon I could tell she was asleep because her breathing had the sleep sound, slow, deep, like it comes from another place than waking breath, lungs way down in your bowels.

I tried to catch my own breathing change, which didn't work until after I woke up from a dream about I couldn't remember what, and my pulse was pumping too hard and my mouth was too dry and June was wrestling with me and telling me to let her go. It was after she settled back down again and I was lying there counting the panes of glass in the window and the pleats in the curtains that I heard the sound of my own breath grow quiet again and felt it cool in my nose.

Cool and quiet breath brought my dream back to me: I was in Covington, in our house, but it was a house full of strangers who answered when I called their names, a stranger named June and a stranger named Caroline and another one named Nate, and each of them was swinging a golf club and hitting the balls at me, at my arms and legs and right up in my face, golf balls bouncing off my elbows and my knees, off my head too, golf ball and bone making a horrible sound, but sound is all there was, no feeling, no pain. I only felt it now, awake, my breath steady still, my sad heart thunderous.

# Chapter 4

Nate used to joke about golf being the highest form of prayer, because no matter how good you got at it, where the ball landed was in God's hands. June liked to pretend it was a sacrilege to say so, but she didn't mean it. We were not a churchgoing family. In fact, Nate was one-quarter Jewish on his mother's side, and he insisted that Jews in particular appreciated the holiness of every daily act, and he figured that meant games too.

Of course, he didn't play golf every day. As far as I could tell, he didn't play every week, or even as often as the weather invited. In fact, what he liked to do best was talk about it. And the thing he liked to do best after that was clean his clubs. For a child of ten, these were the right values. I knew I'd never be invited along to play, but right there at home I was a fine listener and as decent a club cleaner as there was.

We used soap and water on the wooden and metal parts and a damp cloth on the leather, and while we cleaned and polished Nate told me stories about perfect days and perfect greens and perfect martinis drunk in perfect clubhouses in the company of women who were never perfect, because imperfection was what he loved in women, like my gap-toothed smile and my curly black hair.

Sometimes, June would look in on us where we were at our work in the kitchen, or once the weather turned mild, she'd find us sitting out on the back porch. She'd make her yellow ponytail sway with a toss of her head and say something about how she didn't think the trouble we were taking would do shit for Nate's game. When she swore, Nate would swear back. "Your language isn't doing shit for our marriage," he'd say, or, "Your mouth and my game are one perfect damned match."

I use those words and worse today without thinking twice, but back then, God, I loved them—shit, damn, hell—and how you could tell that when people spoke them, they didn't care what anybody thought or what anybody did. I practiced saying them to myself, and sometimes to June, like I did when she caught me with Sarah Siddons one afternoon that summer.

Sarah lived across the street from us in a colonial brick house with a two-car garage. She had perfect teeth and beautiful straight strawberry-blond hair that I coveted and a big brown beauty mark on her chin, which my mother insisted was a mole; just one year older than me, she seemed ages older for all she knew about boys and such.

It was in the week after the Fourth of July. We'd been playing hopscotch on the sidewalk in front of our house when she said she had something good to show me, but we had to go downstairs to our cellar. The next thing I knew, she was standing with her legs spread wide above the drain in the middle of the floor with the hem of her skirt tucked into the waistband, and she was holding her underpants to one side and peeing, and the two of us were giggling from nerves.

She said she saved it up sometimes, because she liked to hear it rush out hard and long when there was a lot of it. She said that was the way boys' pee sounded, and standing up helped. I didn't know about that, but it *was* the longest pee I'd ever seen, and made a loud noise, splashing against the rusty drain cover. She was wiping herself with a piece of newspaper when we heard the door at the top of the stairs open. Then June was at the foot of those stairs in less time than it took Sarah to wad up the piece of paper and set her skirt right again.

"We got a bathroom upstairs for that," my mother said.

"She knows how to use a damned bathroom," I said.

I guess I was both pleased and surprised when Sarah looked at me like swearing was a revelation. She grinned with her finger in her mouth as she tugged at her skirt, and she suddenly looked half my age. But my swearing was no revelation to June, and the smack she landed across my face told me how much I'd better care about what she thought of me. The shadow of her hand on my cheek was red behind my eyes and the sting made my ears ring. I thought my molars would break I clenched my jaws so hard, and the pain shot all the way from my shoulder down to my fingertips. I wanted to swear at her till I made her head spin and hit her right back in her face. I also wanted to plead with her to treat me nice, to reach my arms out to her and know she'd want me.

Caroline was making soup. I could hear her knife on the wooden board and smell the onions as I scrambled up the steps and opened the door into the kitchen. I took my plea and my reaching to her, because I knew she'd welcome them. And she did, she set her knife down, gathered me up in her arms, kissed my stinging cheek and held me against her, as June marched Sarah Siddons up the stairs, through the kitchen and out the back door.

I could see my friend through the window already halfway across the yard when Caroline said, "Lily's cheek's red."

"She swore at me so I hit her," June said.

"She's God's child and Nate doesn't like for you to hit her," Caroline said, and she smoothed the cuff of my sleeve and patted my collar.

"He doesn't like for you to mix her up either, all tender one minute, next minute crazy for God and the holy firmament."

"Just for starters, I never said a word about any firmament," Caroline said, tightening her hold on me. "But besides that, given the choice, I bet Nate'd want to know Lily got plenty of love."

"Given the choice," June replied, "I bet he'd want to know just what you think love is." It was a question I myself didn't dare ask, but just the same I thought it was some kind of answer when June left the room and, a short while later, the house.

After she was gone I helped Caroline with the soup, dropping the carrots and potatoes into the pot, waiting for her to turn wild the way she sometimes did, hoping she'd be nice. And nice she was, holding my hand to show me how much salt to add when the soup was done, giving me her saddest look when I flinched at her quick reach for a rag to catch a spill.

At supper it was just me and her, no word from June, the hour late and us too hungry to wait. Then we played double solitaire till way past my bedtime, and every time Caroline lost a game, she'd say, "Damn it to hell." We'd laugh so hard we'd nearly cry and then I'd say it too, "Damn it all to hell," and before we were through there was playing cards scattered all over the dining room floor and we were dancing jigs and polkas and do-si-dos like a couple of hicks. Then we sat down to a big plate of saltines and strawberry jam. Later she sent me off to bed, my pillow fat under my head, "Paper Roses" soft on her transistor radio from the floor below.

★

When Nate did play golf, it was with a man named Sam Lovell. They'd been to school together, at the Virginia Military Institute in Lexington, only Nate never finished and Sam did. On the other hand, Nate got married and Sam never did. He lived on the other side of town in a house his mother owned, and he worked in a bank.

Nate said Sam Lovell played the worst game of golf in Covington, but he didn't mind, because it wasn't really for the golf that he sought Sam out. It was for the business advice he offered, free of charge. June said as long as Nate was working for somebody else, she couldn't see that he had any need of business advice. Nate said just because he'd been selling James Venery Victor's line for the last ten years didn't necessarily mean he hadn't other ideas. June gave him half a smile and said she had some ideas of her own, some ideas Sam Lovell never heard of. Nate winked at her and said that Sam was a lot sharper than she gave him credit for. June said she'd keep that in mind.

One Sunday that fall, when the two of them, Nate and Sam, had finished up at the nine-hole course at Sam's country club, my father brought his friend home for a drink. They were both wearing loud plaid pants, but Nate's fit him good. Sam's were too tight, so the extra weight he carried around his waist was split in two, making one roll that spilled over his belt and another that pushed out below.

When they walked in, Caroline was taking a nap upstairs and June had just finished polishing our nails at the dining-room table. Mine were bright pink and hers were a pearly shade of orange. Nate went into the kitchen to get some ice and glasses and Sam sat down beside June, who was sipping iced tea through a straw and then blowing cold air on her fingertips.

"I'm next," Sam said.

"What color do you want?" June said with a grin.

"What color do you think, Lily?" he said to me.

I looked at his hands. There was a thick line of black under his nails. "You got to wash first," I said.

"Lily, don't be rude," June said.

"She's not being rude," Nate said, as he set a glass of ice down in front of Sam. "Bourbon or rye?" he asked his friend. Sam answered bourbon and Nate poured. "She's just telling the truth. Anyway, there's nothing wrong with getting your hands a little dirty. And say, listen," he added in Sam's direction, "I think red is your color. Lily, look in the refrigerator where your mama keeps her nail polish and bring out the red."

I'd never seen a man with color on his nails. I'd never even noticed how big a man's fingernails were—almost twice as wide as June's, and thick like a bone. And then that red enamel painted on with so many of June's careful strokes I thought she'd have to use up the whole bottle on just his right hand alone.

She started with Sam's thumb, holding it between her fingers like she did mine. He closed his eyes and let his head fall backward and I could see his pulse popping at the base of his throat. He swallowed hard every now and then, took a sip from his glass and swallowed again. I knew what he was feeling, how even though he was sitting down, each stroke of the brush made him weak in the knees, just like it did mine, and how the polish made the pads of his fingers so sensitive they could feel the finest dust, and even the light from the sun setting outside the dining-room window.

June pushed back the tough cuticle on each finger and studied each nail like it was a puzzle. She sucked on her straw, but all the tea and melted ice were gone from her glass. Nate was telling us about their game, something about the fifth hole, a sand trap, but nobody was listening. He poured June some bourbon and gave himself another shot and then he jumped when Sam coughed. June drank her bourbon through the straw. I chewed the side of my cheek and my bottom lip, first one and then the other, and nobody spoke, as if we all were hypnotized by June's miraculous application of red lacquer to Sam's fingernails.

"All done," June finally said, and she pointed Sam to the mirror above the breakfront. "Take a look at yourself, Mr. Lovell. If it was a matter of hands, you'd make as good a woman as me."

Sam's almost soundless laugh shook his whole body, so he had to hold himself with his arms, though he was careful not to smudge the polish on his shirt and trousers, as he stood in front of the mirror. Nate laughed so hard his pretty green eyes teared, and June's laugh was almost as big, and sweeter than I'd ever heard it before. I tried to laugh like her, but it came out funny, and then they all laughed at me. After a while though, I don't think anybody remembered what we were laughing at, it was like an epidemic of glee that we kept passing back and forth.

Then we heard Caroline on the stairs and Sam looked for some place to hide his hands. But my grandmother spotted them first thing. "Sam Lovell in drag," she tittered. I didn't know what drag meant, but I knew it was okay, because the laughing started up again, and I wished the rest of my life could be just like that, no distance at all between me and the people I loved, so there was even room for someone I didn't.

June and me hated the weekends when Nate was away, and that was at least two times every month. She said it was much worse in the winter, the cold was bad for her concentration, she had no mind for reading or doing crosswords, and the sight of fresh-fallen snow and long winter nights made the romance in her turn sour, because where the hell was he and what in God's name was she saving herself for?

The one thing Nate's absence was good for was bowling, a game he never liked even when he *was* home, so June and me would stop in sometimes at the duck-pin lanes down in the basement of the building where the Covington Rotary Club met. Saturday mornings it was quiet, except for the crackle from the radio that the colored boy listened to when he wasn't setting up pins for the men who bowled a few frames before lunch.

I liked that long dark room that smelled of sweat and paste wax, and I liked those dense black balls. I loved to listen to them as they rolled down the lane and I loved to scream at the crash of the pins when they exploded against each other and fell to the floor.

By the time I was eleven years old, I could bring down enough pins to bother June. "Slow ball like you roll," she said, "beats me how you ever score at all."

"Just wait till I get up some speed," I warned her.

"I'm not ever waiting for you, Lily," she said. "I figure you'll catch up with me some time while I'm resting."

I pretended I didn't hear her say that, pretended I didn't wonder if not waiting for me could somehow turn into leaving without me.

After we played our last frame, we'd sit at one of the little tables that faced the alleys and share a cold soda the boy served us from a round red tray. June would pay him with a few coins she'd drop into his hand. The boy always said thank you and June always said he was mighty welcome. Then the two of them would smile. I smiled too and I remember this one time the boy's eyes shifted real slow from my mother to me and he smiled a little harder but his eyes weren't smiling, they were going inside me, just like Nate's eyes did, and it shook me so that I hardly noticed when, with his free hand, he reached toward me—to pet my head? to brush my cheek?—but June said, "Don't you dare," in a voice that *was* a dare every bit as much as it was a warning, and the boy's hand stopped halfway to where I was already feeling his touch.

"Nice-looking boy," June said when he'd turned and walked back to the kitchen. "Too bad he's a negro. Nice looking just the same."

At the time I didn't wonder how my mother could live life so close to the edge, but in later years I figured it had something to do with a game she liked to play, and the men around her, the boys just as well, and some other women, white with colored and colored with white, they liked to play it too. They liked seeing how much they could get away with without it costing them too much, everybody always trying to gauge the differences between them in might and will and allure. It was a game I stayed shy of, at least for a time, but that Sam Lovell was a player.

Late that spring, just after I'd beat June with a strike in the last frame, Sam stopped at the door and waved. June put her arm around me where we were sitting and drinking a grape pop. I nestled against her and felt her skin grow hot and damp through her dress when Sam blew her a kiss. "Blow him a kiss, honey," June said to me, and I did. "Isn't that man a perfect sweetheart?" she whispered. Of course that man was the last thing on my mind. I was thinking about how me and June fit together so good and how her heat made a melting place between us, but I said yes just the same.

Another time, I said no. We were standing in the checkout line at the grocery store, I was looking at the candy bars and June was reading something to me from a magazine. Sam came up behind us and said boo. I hated that, for a grown man to talk baby talk. "Did I scare you?" he asked June.

"I don't scare easy, but Lily does, don't you, Sugar?" she said.

"Hell, no," I said, and I made my selection from the candy display—I guarantee it was chocolate—and set it in among the bottles of milk and the eggs and apples.

"Put that right back, young lady," June snarled.

"Oh, June, let her have it," Sam said. "Give it here, girlie, I'll buy it for you."

"No thank you," I said, and I put the candy back in the box on the shelf.

Then it was our turn to pay for our groceries, and June pointed to the box of laundry soap Sam was holding. "You've just got the one item," she said. "Why don't you go ahead of us?"

"We're in an awful hurry," I reminded June, but then I couldn't remember why, so when she asked me, I made something up. June laughed and gave Sam a little nudge. He pushed past us, paid for his soap, said his good-byes, and headed for the door.

"You weren't very nice to him," June said, putting our groceries on the counter.

"I know," I said, "I'm sorry."

"Are you?"

"Uh-huh."

"Do you know you have your daddy's smile?"

"I do."

"Would you like a package of chewing gum?"

I picked Juicy Fruit because it was the sweetest, and I hoped with every stick that the flavor wouldn't turn dull in minutes the way my mother's sweet regard could turn in an instant to favor somebody else. But it did. That's why when we were halfway home and June asked me if I could spare her a piece of gum, I'd already gone through the whole package.

★

Nate said he couldn't chew and smoke at the same time, so when he smoked he sucked on hard candies, mint-flavored mostly, but every now and then, he'd get a taste for butterscotch. June said the smell of butterscotch candy was enough to turn her three shades of green, especially when the weather was hot.

That summer the heat did what it always did, slipped down the side of the mountain and settled into the Covington valley like it was home. I read books about the North Pole and drew pictures of avalanches. June set pans of water all over the house for us to dunk our feet in, and she left towels hanging over the backs of chairs for drying off. She said wetting your feet had a cooling effect. Caroline said sweating was the best way to cool off. She wore heavy socks and thick-soled shoes and wrapped her head in one of Nate's old T-shirts like the colored people in town did and June said wasn't it exactly like Caroline to take on the ways of the colored and Caroline said exactly.

Nate called from Radford one Friday night in August to say he was having car trouble. The mechanic said he'd work on it in the morning, so Nate could make it home by suppertime Saturday. June dabbed her damp forehead and said never mind, why didn't she just this once hop a bus and meet him in Radford for the weekend. He said no, that didn't make sense, and besides, he wanted to see me. When she hung up the telephone, she kicked at one of the kitchen chairs. "Did you ever hear of a garage that plays church music on the radio?"

When he called again in the morning, I was helping Caroline hang out the wash. "Come pick up the telephone," June hollered to me in the backyard.

He didn't even ask to speak to my mother. He sang me the chorus to "No Other Love," but when I joined in he cut me off because he only had a half minute, he was out of change, there was somebody else waiting to use the telephone and there was just enough time to ask me if I knew how much he loved me with a little time left over for me to say how much I loved him back. Then with his last breath he said, "Tell your mama the car's busted. I'll give you a call during the week, and I'll be home real soon."

It doesn't take much for a child to make her father a hero: I simply believed him. But June didn't. So I had to put a lot of distance between us in order to protect my belief. Then she made it real easy and called Sam Lovell that very instant, said she was looking for some amusement, promised she'd bring the red nail polish.

She didn't come home for dinner. Caroline and me roasted corn and potatoes in the barbecue pit behind the garage. It was so hot inside the house that she said we ought to sleep on the porch. We could take our showers under the spray from the hose right there in the garden—there was no moon to give us away.

She lit a couple of citronella candles and turned on the spigot. Our clothes were ghostly piles on the grass. The crickets sawed and the ground turned to mud and the wind came up and blew out the candles. Caroline scooped up the mud in her hands and spread it all over her arms and her legs and her skin turned black. I sang the verse to "No Other Love" and strained my eyes to see hers, but I couldn't make them out. I stopped straining when I felt her cold fingers on my ankles, and I watched myself disappear.

When we were both covered from head to toe, Caroline said to stand still so the mud could dry without cracking. It grabbed at my skin like something pulling at me gently. The wind whipped up a frenzy in the trees and my skin shrunk around me and I felt afraid. "Mud's got spirits in it," Caroline said. "Can you feel 'em talking to you?"

"Whose spirits?" I asked her.

"Everybody's," she said. "In the spirit world, there's no separation, no difference between Jew and gentile, between colored and white, between child and elder or man and woman."

This was a notion I could not comprehend, though it had an affect on me just the same, the way big ideas sometimes come to your body and not your brain: up behind my eyes and all down my spine I felt a cold white light like the flashing tilt signs on a pinball machine.

Caroline grabbed me by the arms. "Child, you're shaking all over," she said. She pulled me to her and I could feel her cold and my cold touching, or was it the spirits? She brushed the dried mud from my face and neck, and then from my arms, and her hands were smooth and warm. We were cold and we were hot and I got dizzy from the chill and the fever and when my legs gave out from under me, she picked me up and carried me in her arms.

She spread an old sheet on the back porch glider. Her stomach was big between us, her breasts were like empty old paper bags, made soft from use. I was crying, but I thought she couldn't hear me. "Shhhhh," she whispered, and she gave a little push so we began to swing. The springs creaked and the floorboards groaned and Caroline sang, "No other love have I," and I cried harder, for fear, for sorrow, in awe, the world too big for me, difference all I knew.

In the morning, June found me dirty in my bed between sheets streaked with dried mud. "What on earth happened to you?" she said. "Don't tell me your grandmother made you the mess you are this morning. Didn't I tell you to stay out of her way?"

I tapped my foot and sifted dried mud between my fingers. June said she'd strip my bedsheets while I cleaned myself up and put on some clothes. Then we were going to walk into town for breakfast because there was no coffee and no eggs, and she wasn't in the mood to do the marketing.

Along the way, she told me how she'd got Sam to drive her to Radford. They spent three hours looking for Nate's car, and finally found it parked in front of a motel room just outside of town. Sam wanted her to stay in the car, in fact he wanted her to hide on the floor of the backseat, that was his plan, because now that they'd found Nate, Sam would just as soon his friend didn't know he had the Mrs. with him. After all, how would it look? So he'd knock on the door, and when Nate answered, he'd say he just happened to be in the area and noticed the Chevrolet. But, no sir, June said, if anybody was going to knock on that door, it would be her, never mind how it looked.

Even before Nate answered her knock, she could hear radio church music coming from inside the room. When he opened the door, he had his arm around a woman who was half undressed, down to her slip and stockings, and her hair undone, and all he said was Jesus Christ, June, was she satisfied?

"And really," June said to me where we stood waiting for a traffic light to change, "that was it."

Of course there was other things said among them, which June told me about while we ate our fried eggs and toast at the diner: Nate told Sam to take June home, Sam said the whole thing was a big mistake, June said maybe it wasn't. But those were just the things that had to be said to get everybody along to what came next, which was Nate closing the door and June and Sam getting back in Sam's car and driving to the next motel. That's where they spent the night, because it was too late to drive back to Covington. But June said she was up early in the morning and she wanted to get right on the road, the motel wasn't air-conditioned and the heat was unbearable in that stuffy little room, worse yet for the smell of Sam's aftershave. "Single men always use too much scent," she said. "At least in the car you can roll the windows down and get some air."

She sipped her tea, put a quarter in the little jukebox at our booth and punched in three Jo Stafford songs, and when the first one started she looked at me real close. "You still got dirt on your face," she said. "What the hell happened to you last night?"

I didn't answer her that time either, because I was caught in a vicious spiderweb among the three of them, June, Nate, and Caroline: no one of them alone was a sure bet, but maybe all of them together was. So I just tapped my foot some more and tried to look cross and sang along with Jo. After a while, June told me to wipe my face and asked the waitress to pour her some more hot water. Then she said we'd better go home so she could start packing Nate's things, because she damned sure wasn't having him living in that house.

I don't know what would have come of it all if Nate's brakes hadn't failed on a hairpin turn just outside of Pulaski. It was only a couple of hours later when they called to say he was being operated on that very minute and Sam drove me and June to the hospital and everybody cried.

Nate had to recover at home for six months, both legs in casts for three, then there was crutches and canes. For six months, my mother occupied my father as though he was her job, and my father let her—there was no attention but hers he wanted, no consideration of mine that mattered, no meeting between our eyes, no deeper sighting then or ever again. Caroline went to stay the winter with a distant relative in Pennsylvania and I turned to Sarah Siddons' big sister Katie, who taught me words with more punch than anything I'd heard at home and when the words weren't bad enough, we watched her brothers Lewis and Howard in the barn with a girl named Portia and they brought the words to life, the boys' bare butts rising and falling atop her, me and Katie red in the face with our fingers in our underpants, Caroline's wild calling loud inside my head—hadn't I once seen her doing it too, where was it? Sitting in the bathtub doing just that way, rubbing herself like she was scrubbing a stain from her flesh, then suddenly her whole body jerking like mine, like a wild turkey plugged with buckshot.

# Chapter 5

Vero Beach was the first time I'd seen the Atlantic Ocean or set my feet in such fine sand and June let me get my fill. It was well into October, but the water was still warm. I stood close to the shore where the waves lapped at my legs, and I could see the hairs on my calves skitter in the water like little fishes and the air was soft on my skin, full of the taste and the smell of the sea.

June told me to take the Band-Aids off my fingers because the saltwater would help my scraped knuckles heal. I did, and it stung at first, but then it felt good and June said how beautiful I looked with the sun on my face. We stared up at the tall palm trees and watched pelicans dive for dinner just a few feet from the shore. June bought me a glass of orange juice squeezed fresh by a man on the boardwalk and she said she was feeling better and I said I was too.

Starting the very next day, she took a job packing fruit a few miles out of town, she said it wasn't the kind of work she liked but it would do for a while. And we got a room at a resort motel for cheap because it was still off-season and the place was a little run-down. But they had a saltwater swimming pool and a snack bar, which is where we ate a lot of our meals, and I guess June had had something in mind for us all along, because after we'd been there just one night and one day, she said that the woman who ran the snack bar was Nate's stepsister and my aunt, Beulah Younger. But she didn't want to let on to her who we were until we'd had a chance to see what kind of person she was. Then, if it turned out we liked her, and if she had herself a nice arrangement and was willing to help out family, even if we were only related by marriage and even though she'd never met either one of us, then June would find a way to let it slip who we were, and everything would fall into place.

Beulah Younger was nearly six feet tall, but she was stoop-shouldered, like she regretted her height, something I was sure Nate Wolsey never did, and her tiny brown eyes looked sightless behind the thick lenses of her eyeglasses. How I did scrutinize that woman, looking for some trace of my father in her, and finding none I missed him more, finding none I set myself against her, though against her meant against my mother too.

Every morning before June left for the packing plant, we'd go over to the snack bar for breakfast. Beulah would prepare and serve our order and ask had we had a good night's sleep and June always said something clever like the further south she got the better she slept. Then Beulah would say something like Florida was about as far south as you could go. "What about Mexico and Argentina?" I'd ask.

June praised Beulah's pancakes, I faulted them—they were burnt around the edges and raw in the middle. June laughed at Beulah's jokes, I made a sour face—they were corny, they were dumb. June invited Beulah on a picnic, I walked on the beach by myself and threw broken bits of shells at the gulls.

June took Beulah to the hairdresser for a new style, I laughed at her feather cut teased into the middle of next week. In some unknowing way, I was determined to reject the woman, and make her heir to all the hurt and anger Nate had caused me, it being, as I see it now, far safer to hate someone who meant nothing to me than someone who might have meant everything.

There *was* one thing about Beulah that nearly redeemed her in my eyes—she read the stars. She studied books and charts that told her what was to come in the lives of everyone ever born. June never wanted anything to do with Beulah's astrology, though she tried to be polite and listen so as not to give offense. Beulah sensed it just the same, and didn't make too much of it when June was around. But I thought she'd give me a look at my future, so I kept my mouth shut, hoping that I'd get an earful once we were installed in her house a few miles west of town.

That's where we lived after June said in passing one morning that we were from Virginia, a little nothing of a town, maybe Beulah'd heard of it, Covington. Before that, my mother had talked about home, but she'd saved the name of the place for just the right moment. That was the same morning she said that her estranged husband was not just "the man I'm married to" or "Lily's daddy." He had a name, Nate, and we were Wolseys, not just June and Lily.

Beulah raised her hands up in the air like she was going to sing hallelujah and after there was all kinds of explanations made and stories told, Beulah said, "That Nathaniel is only my stepbrother—you know we just met a time or two, but he is surely my kin, so there's to be no discussion, you're coming home with me, right now. They'll have to make their own sandwiches."

June called in sick at the packing plant and we collected

our things from our room. We were taking a last look in the bureau drawers and closets when I asked what it meant if somebody was your stepbrother.

"Beulah's mother and father divorced when she was grown and gone from home," June explained. "Nate was the child of her daddy's second wife, long before he married her." That she hardly knew my father and that there was no blood between us explained a lot of things to me, especially my natural dislike of the woman.

About the time we settled in at their house, Beulah's sons said there was work on their shift at the fruit-packing plant and Beulah took her vacation. So June went to work with the Younger boys—Lyman was the quiet one, and Torrence was the hell-raiser, Lyman played chess and Torrence played trumpet, Lyman was the one who loved his mother and Torrence was the one his mother loved—and Beulah stayed home and talked to me about the zodiac. She told me that my sun was in Aries, and that I had Pisces rising. I didn't know what the Aries or the Pisces parts meant, but I loved the rising part. I loved to picture myself that way, rising up. I also loved the way she talked about *my* moon and *my* Mars and *my* Venus, like I had one of each that was my very own, and it didn't bother me in the least that everybody else had one too.

"What about my future?" I asked her.

She studied her charts some more. "Well, the news isn't good and it isn't bad," she reported as she closed her book.

"What does it say?" I asked her.

"Says any day now, you're going to find yourself caught halfway between making something of yourself and making a real wreck of things."

"What the hell does that mean?"

She made a woeful face and worried the corner of her

book. "Means you've got to grow up fast and make up your mind what you want, Lily, you got to choose."

"Between what and what?"

"Between what you're given and what you create."

I thought I'd never heard such a lot of hooey, I figured June was right, the woman didn't know shit from Shineola, with her stooped shoulders and her little eyes swimming like black beans behind her eyeglasses, so I got up from the kitchen table and I marched right out of the house.

Most days I thought the sky was too big there in Florida and the land was too flat without the mountains I'd always known, so it all looked stripped bare, and it made me feel bare too. But then that one day, feeling bare as that land, I loved my stride too big and my face stretched wide and that merciless Florida sun so hot on my head. Walking aimlessly down dirt roads and farm lanes, I saw colored children sucking on sugarcane and a bunch of men cooking something on a little gas stove beside a pickup truck and one old, red-skinned man patching tires beside a shack on the bank of an irrigation ditch.

The old man said he had a long Indian name nobody could pronounce, so everybody called him Polly. His thick black hair hung heavy as a drape from a weathered black felt hat, but you could still see he was wall-eyed. I said Polly didn't seem a proper name for a man, and he said thank you, that was just the point, he wasn't known for acting proper and I spent the rest of the day flirting with him, playing shy, lending a hand, talking dirty Katie Siddons talk, right up until Lyman came looking for me to tell me it was time for supper.

"I'm not hungry," I said to him.

"Come on back to the house anyway," he said. "No place for a nice girl here." He must have been about twenty-five years old, tall and gangly, with his mother's little eyes and

skinny lips that made him look like he'd swallowed his
mouth. He kept his hands in his pockets as he shuffled his
weight from one foot to the other like the ground was no
sure thing. "There's tapioca pudding," he said and he smiled
like he thought tapioca pudding was divine. Then he added,
"I made it myself." He was a grown man desperate for affection—you could see it in the way he stared at his shoes, like
he was afraid to look up and find your eyes someplace else—
and I guess I felt sorry for him, so I let him take my hand and
I liked how he shortened his stride to match mine and we
took the long way home so we could buy a pint of heavy
cream to whip for the pudding and I didn't say a word about
how I wasn't a nice girl.

With June bringing home extra money for our room and
board, Beulah quit her job at the motel snack bar and kept
house for the four of us. I was registered in the sixth grade at
Vero Beach Middle School and I rode the bus every morning
with the scraggly children of white migrant farm workers,
children who looked like they had no futures at all, for which
I both loved and hated them.

Among the ones I loved and hated best was a girl named
Charlene Sipp, small and clean and refined as a migrant's
child could be. I loved her for the lisp that made her *s* words
sound like whistles and for her slim fingers that looked so
delicate tying her shoelaces or peeling a banana. I hated her
for the hopeless mess she made of her homework papers and
how the blood rose up in her face when the teacher called her
name.

"Charlene, who was the first man to set foot in Florida?"

Her blue eyes beseeched me to tell her the answer, but I
turned my back and counted to three. Then I raised my hand
and spoke at the same time. "Ponce de Leon," I said, "gov-
ernor of Puerto Rico, in 1513."

"You don't have to talk out of turn, Lily," the teacher said. But I did. I had to shout out the answer or it would shatter my brain, just like the sight of Charlene did, a wretched lump in her chair, her pretty fingers drumming nervous messages to no one on the leg of her desk.

Sometimes, when I wasn't angry with her, I'd bring Charlene home for supper. One night after we'd eaten too much of Beulah's veal loaf and rice and gravy, my aunt asked her when her birthday was and Charlene named the date. The next morning when we were cleaning up after breakfast, my aunt said there was no sense saying anything about it to the girl, but the stars told a sad story about my little friend.

Lyman and Torrence had taken their cups of coffee outside, where they were working on one of their cars, but June was right there with us in the kitchen when Beulah gave her report. Me and my mother just rolled our eyes, even though a lot of the time I wasn't talking to her and when I did it was usually to cuss and swear or tell her a lie or speak some vicious insult to her, which was sometimes true and sometimes not and I didn't care, because she only came home to bathe and change her clothes and order me around. The rest of the time she was either at work with the Younger brothers or out honky-tonking with Torrence and his friends—convertible cars, beach parties, loud music from a radio or sometimes Torrence played his trumpet and somebody else played the harmonica, wild nights in a rich man's lemon groves that she'd tell me about when she got home. One time I called her a whore and she smacked me in my face. I didn't mind. I was so glad to feel the hurt for real, glad to have something real to cry over, and if it ended with me sobbing her name and Nate's and Caroline's into my pillow, then I didn't mind that either.

"Too bad you got such a mouth on you, Lily," she said. "I

was going to take you with me next time, but the way you talk I wouldn't take you to hell."

I told my mother she hadn't heard anything yet and I ignored Beulah's predictions about Charlene, who saved her pennies until she had a quarter, and then she asked me to go with her to the five-and-dime photo booth. I stared into the flashing light and a couple of minutes later, a strip of four pictures of us dropped out of the slot. In every picture Charlene was looking at me like I was the stars in her eyes, while I was looking at the camera, flint-faced and cold. She offered to share the pictures with me, to cut the strip in half so we could each have two. I said why didn't we keep all the pictures together, she could have them for the first year, I'd take them for the year after, and we could keep switching back and forth. But the truth was I didn't ever want to see those pictures again, didn't want to see myself that way, my dark eyes fixed in a stare and my mouth set like a swath of misery across my face.

Besides Charlene, there was a boy from Macon named Lucas who said he chose me for my black hair and my green eyes and I let him. He was two years ahead of me in school and according to Beulah, he was a double Scorpio and that was double trouble. I *did* wonder if my aunt knew how me and him carried on in the Buick every chance we got, waiting till June went out with Torrence, climbing into the backseat of our car, touching each other, just through our clothes at first, but then we'd unbutton and unzip till we looked like the ravages of sale day at the department store.

After we finished, he'd tell me stories about what he'd done before, once he told me he had an uncle who fiddled with him—that's what he called it. I told him about Kate and Lewis and Howard Siddons and what I'd seen Caroline do in the tub and how I tried it myself sometimes. Did I like it? he wanted to know and I said I did and I didn't, because it excited me but it scared me too, like I was coming apart and coming together at the same time.

Lucas said I was making something very simple sound very complicated and he changed the subject, which was easy for him because he was such a talented boy. He could juggle five balls, count to one hundred in three foreign languages, and recite the speeches of Abraham Lincoln like he was thinking them up on the spot. He tried to teach me to juggle, but I couldn't manage more than two balls, and I learned some numbers in French and Spanish, but I never got to one hundred or German. Mostly he just laughed at my failures, but once in frustration, he asked me, "What *can* you do?"

"I can cuss good," I said.

"That's no big deal," he said. "Anyway, so can I."

"I can sing," I said.

"Oh boy," he said, "let's hear it," and he sat up straight and looked all ears. I was set to sing him something pretty, I was five bars into "Three Coins in the Fountain," but then he was grinning at me and pulling on himself and I said I'd just as soon sing to the devil and I walked off and left him.

I wanted to stay mad at Lucas when he carried on that way, but the truth was I couldn't afford it. June was always going off, to Miami now or Palm Beach or Naples, with Torrence and his friends—overnight, whole weekends—and leaving me notes filled with row after row of hugs and kisses—

XOXOXOXOXOXOXOXOXOX
XOXOXOXOXOXOXOXOXOX

—which she never, *ever*, delivered when she came home with sand in her shoes. Not that I'd have had them, her hugs and kisses, not that I wanted them one bit.

Beulah seemed to take it as a sign that, with my mother

gone so much of the time, she was next in line for the job. Unfortunately, her idea of mothering was like something pesky buzzing in your ear. So I paid her no mind when she worried about my comings and goings, but I let her iron my blouses and cook my favorite meals, fried catfish and banana fritters, Brunswick stew and cornbread, and I kept my mouth shut about how much my mother's absence troubled me, and how our room seemed so big with her gone, even though when she was there the thing I wished for most was a room of my own.

Lyman seemed to know and share my distress, I guess because my mother going off without me was just a bigger version of what he got from Beulah: he brought her presents, lavender oil, fresh flowers, and she could barely manage to thank him; he went with her to church and she'd take a seat and then after he sat beside her, she'd get up and move to another pew. But if the fuss she made over me made him jealous, he never said a word about it, and we still kept each other company plenty of times, my schoolwork and his chess game, me staring off at nothing with my history book in my lap opened to the wrong chapter, Lyman staring off somewhere else with a pawn or a castle gripped tight in his fist.

Early that winter Charlene told me they were having tryouts for the girls' choir, why didn't we go, they gave out free cookies and milk after practice. We went and they said no to Charlene but they said yes to me.

I sang with the altos so I had to memorize the harmony to dozens of songs I already knew. Soon it got to where I couldn't remember the melodies I'd sung all my life and it worried me so that once or twice I'd forget myself and ask June, when she was at home for some reason or other, if she'd sing "Bless This House" and "In the Cool, Cool, Cool of the Evening," just so I could hear the tunes. She'd start right in, nodding at her hands folded in her lap like she was thinking about some other time, and then, because I couldn't resist it—because I couldn't resist her—I'd come in with that alto line.

We'd be sitting at Beulah's kitchen table or on the double bed we shared in our room, and we'd turn to face each other in those duets till I didn't know who was singing which part, didn't know which voice was mine and which was hers. But it always ended with me getting up and walking out in the middle of a chorus and June calling where was I going and what in God's name was wrong with me and sometimes I'd call back that there wasn't a damned thing wrong with me, and other times I'd say I didn't know. But I knew. I hated loving her because I hated what she made of my love: an old pair of shoes, worn and run-down at the heels, good for tramping around the house and taking out the garbage, not meant for dressing up and showing off and good times.

Choir practice was Tuesday and Thursday afternoons, and I never missed one. I couldn't complain when they had me stand in the back row of five, because I was that tall. I stood up to my full height and I shaped my vowels just like they showed us and I thought I had somehow distinguished myself, so I was mad as hell when they didn't give me a solo in the Easter concert, and I didn't invite June, because I didn't want her to see me hidden, my voice lost among all those other girls'.

Charlene was there, though, and so was Lucas. For the most part they hadn't much use for each other, but that day they made some kind of peace and when the concert was over, Lucas took us out for ice cream. Charlene was all thank yous and slurps, licking her spoon and sucking up every bit of her strawberry soda from the bottom of her glass. When she finished, she said it was the first ice-cream soda she'd ever had. Like I couldn't bear the ease among us or her simple ways, I told her that was a load of bull and why did she make herself out to be so pitiful. Lucas told me to shut up, why would she lie and what the hell did I know about pity anyway? Then he put some change on the counter, grabbed Charlene by the hand and walked out of the drugstore. I sat at that counter for a long while, drank a couple of glasses of water, watched an old lady eat a piece of banana cream pie, watched the soda jerk clean the grill.

It was late by the time I got back to Beulah's, Torrence and Lyman's cars gone from the driveway, a pile of wet towels on the floor in the bathroom, my mother's work clothes strewn about our room. Beulah's bedroom door was open, her big back was humped where she sat on the bed poring over her star books.

I could hear somebody's radio a few houses away. I followed Frankie Lane's faint voice out of the house and then I left that voice behind and turned toward where the Buick was parked under a big mimosa tree at the far end of the driveway. There, sitting on the hood of the car with a lit cigarette to his mouth and the glow flashing orange on his face, was Lucas. I took my time making my way to him. He opened the car door and we climbed into the backseat. He put his arms around me and kissed me once. The tobacco taste of his dry mouth made my head swim. Pictures of my mother and my father came floating up before me, cigarettes and kisses floated up too, and I looked, but I couldn't make out what came next.

*Chapter 6*

Spring came early the year Nate recovered from his accident. It was late April and already my twelfth birthday and the forsythia had come and gone, and the lilacs were in full bloom by the time he was strong enough to drive. He was taking June in the brand-new Buick to some fancy hot springs hotel where society people played golf and tennis and danced the nights away. That's how my mother described it to me where I stood watching her in front of the downstairs hall mirror, posing for all she was worth. She had her hair done up in a French twist, and she was wearing a low-cut white dress with a big skirt and a bunch of white crinolines, and the highest high-heeled shoes I'd ever seen.

"We're having a celebration," she said as she turned around and pointed to the back of her dress.

I pulled up the zipper the last inch and fastened the snap at the top. "What are you celebrating?" I asked.

"Your daddy's recovery," she said, "and me getting out of the house for the first time in too long."

June fussed over Nate when he came downstairs, dressed in

his fresh pressed suit and a tie. In the months he'd been laid up, I'd noticed he'd grown quiet, nearly shy, or else he was doing a lot of thinking; his eyes had dulled and he hardly ever laughed, so it felt to me that even with him there twenty-four hours a day, I was always waiting for him to come home—now that he was stuck in Covington he had what June had, that lust to be somewhere else.

Caroline had returned from Pennsylvania and I'd surprised myself with how happy I was to see her and how glad I was for the gifts she'd brought me, a Robin Hood wristwatch and a pair of roller skates. Now she came out to the hall from the kitchen. "Oh my," she said to Nate and June, "you two look elegant as Nick and Nora Charles. All you need is a little dog to finish the picture."

June fluffed up her skirt and crinolines, which were already as big as a house. "A dog is the last thing I need," she said. She started to fuss with the pocket of my blouse. "There's supper in the fridge, just leftovers, but you don't mind, Honey, do you? And Caroline's going to make something special for dessert."

As it turned out, Caroline didn't make anything at all for dessert. She sat quietly at the dining-room table, listening to her transistor radio turned way down low and pasting stamps into a black album she'd brought home from Harrisburg. I sat on the living-room floor and worked on my mathematics assignment. I had to make a pie chart that showed how many days out of the last 365 had been clear days and how many had been cloudy and how many days it had rained and so on, with big and little slices of the pie for each kind of weather. What a bunch of nonsense. But I did it just the same because Sarah was visiting with her cousins and Katie was home sick with whooping cough and I didn't like to fool with her brothers when she wasn't around and Caroline wasn't making any moves toward the kitchen.

She didn't even answer when I asked what time we could have our supper. In fact it was well past dark by the time I helped myself to some cold meat loaf and egg noodles. After that we watched some TV quiz shows and comedies, though I think my grandmother slept through most of them. When I got tired, I kissed her good night and she kissed me back.

Upstairs, I took my bath and went to bed. I don't know what time it was when I heard the voice of Connie Francis growing louder as my grandmother climbed the stairs. Then I heard the door to the bathroom close and after that I guess I fell back to sleep. It seemed like the middle of the night when I woke up to the sound of her radio again, Pat Boone soft at first and then louder as Caroline walked nearer and nearer to my bedroom door, and I swear to God she stood there like she meant for me to wake and then to listen to her going down the stairs, padding in her house slippers through the kitchen and out the back door.

I got up and stood at the window and watched her dancing slow and sweet to "Love Letters in the Sand," casting long shadows in the light of the full moon. Then she stopped and walked past the garage where there was no Buick in sight and across the back of the yard and on to I didn't know where. So I put on my shoes and a sweater and followed her, through our woods and across a little marsh and down to the pond on our neighbor's land.

She set her radio down on a grassy knoll, stripped herself naked and waded into the pond, stood there knee-deep and played her palms over the surface of the water like she was smoothing out the sheets of a bed, walked a few steps deeper and dropped down until her head disappeared below the glimmering black surface. I don't know how long she stayed under, but it was long enough for me to begin to fear that she might not come up. On the other hand, if it was fear, why did I stay so rooted to the spot, quiet at first, though inside was a deafening roar? Then I was crying, shaking with sobs, my steps small and uncertain as, finally, I made my way to the water's edge and beyond, crying louder now, filled with dread and rage, her name the one word I shrieked.

But when my grandmother rose from the pond, my crying stopped, and, face to face with only the water separating us, I could see the love that lived between us bright as the burning filament of a hundred-watt bulb; I could hear Lewis Siddons calling his brother; I could feel someone coming near, June's silent steps like skin against my skin, and then the sound of twigs snapping and last fall's dead leaves rustling under her feet.

"What the hell are you doing down here with my daughter, you old witch?" my mother screamed.

"Night and day, living and dying, it's all the same," Caroline said as she gave my fingers a quick squeeze and then, laughing, began to splash the water with the heels of her hands, sending big silvery flares of the pond toward me and toward June, who made her way to my side and pulled me to the shore and up into the marsh.

She was crying. I hated that, I had to get her to stop. "Mama, Mama," I said through my own tears and I thought I heard her say it too, "Mama, Mama," as we stumbled back through the woods.

"Stop it, Lily," she snarled, and she half dragged me across our backyard, past the garage where the Buick was parked now, and upstairs to her room.

Nate wasn't there. June's white dress and crinolines were in a heap on the floor, but there was no sign of his suit or his tie or his tiepin and cufflinks in the dish where he always put them. June picked up a framed picture of my father and looked at it and then she threw it across the room. Next thing I knew she was pulling the suitcases down from the closet and throwing things in, her clothes and her jewelry and a few towels. My heart was beating so hard, my worst fears coming to pass right in front of my eyes. "Where are you going?" I asked her, but she didn't answer. She just moved with me to my room and started stuffing my clothes into pillowcases and a quilt cover.

"Help me," she said. "I can't do this alone." So I started stuffing too. She was sobbing and then I was crying harder than ever. "Stop your carrying on, goddamn it," she said.

"Well, you're crying," I said.

"No, I'm not," she said through her tears.

"Yes, you are," I said, crying even more.

She shook me. "Shut up, Lily," she scolded through the choking in her throat. "Shut up, so I don't have to get crazy myself."

What was crazy? I was stomping my feet and drooling and shivering. "What is happening?" I screamed at her. "What is happening?"

She smacked me across the face—I heard it but I didn't feel it—and she shoved a full pillowcase in my arms. "Take this downstairs and put it in the car," she said, "and then come up and get another one, and don't say a single goddamned word, do you hear me?"

We were on the other side of the mountains before either one of us spoke, and even then we started off with the things we always said when we were riding in the car.

"Can we put the heat on?" I asked.

"It's nearly May," she said.

"I'm cold."

"Get me a cigarette from the pack in the glove compartment," she said as she turned a dial on the dashboard.

The heater roared. June kept both hands on the steering wheel and smoked with her cigarette hanging from between her lips and her eyes squinted half shut to keep out the smoke. We hardly ever passed another car, and the sky was still dark and I had the feeling that we were driving into the night like it was a tunnel with no opening at the other end. Then the sky began to pale and I missed the dark, missed how it hid us from sight. At sunup I saw a boy in overalls throwing stones at last year's scarecrow, his back turned to a sick cow with her thick, black tongue hanging out of her mouth and her eyes popping out of her head like her brains were bursting. Along the roadside, billboards advertised farm insurance, a hot-dog stand, an Oldsmobile dealer. I think now I was looking at everything so I could remember it, so the memories of the boy and the billboards would take up all the room there was in my mind, leaving no place for the things I didn't want there, broken glass and Nate's picture on the bedroom floor and Caroline standing stark naked beside the garage, laughing with her mouth open wide and her hands gripped tight at her bare breasts and June's wail, a lonely echo of my own from the inside of the car as we closed and locked the doors.

Somewhere around Bluefield, we stopped for gas. Inside the filling station where you paid, they sold canned goods and pigs' feet in brine and off in one corner there was a dozen smoked hams hanging from a wire stretched between two nails, each ham dressed in a white net sock.

"You think we should take a ham to Sally and Neil?" June said, coming up behind me.

Without even turning around to look at her I said, "Where's Nate?"

"I can't remember eating ham at their house," she went on. "Some people are funny about pork."

"Where is he?" I said, a good deal louder this time.

"Maybe we should just bring them a big jar of honey."

"Tell me, Mama," I hollered.

She smacked me across the face. This time I felt the sting, and then my ears were buzzing and my nose started running and I was hot inside my clothes. I reached up to smack her back and she seized my hand with a fierce grip. "I left him at the hotel," she said.

"Why?"

"Because he told me to."

"What do you mean?"

"He said for me to go home, to take the car and drive myself on home."

"No, he didn't."

"Listen to me," she said, and she shook my chin and made me look right at her. Her lips trembled and twitched, and there was all kinds of words being spoken behind her eyes, but she didn't say a one of them. She just stood there like that, and me with her. Then she let go of my chin and said, "Never mind."

# Chapter 7

It was so cold that winter in Florida they lost almost the whole citrus crop. June said wasn't it just our luck to come south for the coldest winter of the century. With hardly any fruit to juice for freezing or canning, she, Torrence, and Lyman were laid off from the processing plant. So they went to work with the pickers, whites and coloreds and some Spanish too, trying to ward off the killing frost, covering the trees with countless yards of muslin and setting smudge pots among the thousands of rows of grapefruits and oranges.

Toward the end of February, Lyman fell from a ladder and broke his arm. He wasn't in much pain, but he wasn't much use in the groves, so Beulah said he might as well stay home and let her take care of him. There with them after school, watching her bring him tuna-fish sandwiches and bowls of potato chips, I got the feeling that he was right where he wanted to be, but I could also tell that Beulah wished it was Torrence who'd fallen, because she'd have liked his company better than Lyman's. She'd have preferred the dirty jokes and the crude humor of her oldest boy to the quiet of her youngest, though I did notice now he was only quiet when his mother was around. When she'd go out to the store or across town to visit a friend, he was like a different person, friendly, thoughtful, asking could he help me with my homework and did I want to have a piece of coffee cake with him? More often than not I said yes, but then sitting beside him on the couch parsing sentences or picking walnuts from the sugary frosting, I wished I was off somewhere with Charlene or Lucas.

Dressed in heavy work trousers and somebody's old jacket, with a kerchief around her head and gloves in her pockets, June still went over to the groves every morning with Torrence, and they stayed on way past dark, sharing with the coloreds and the Spanish and the whites cup after cup of hot coffee from thermoses the bosses kept full, and the beer and cheap wine somebody always had hidden in the backseat of an old jalopy. But the fruit turned black on the branches and they lost most of the crop. When spring came, Torrence said the hell with it, if he couldn't make things better he was going to make them worse.

"How much worse could things be?" Beulah asked one night at supper. "Not a single one of you employed, government checks not more than a pittance, mortgage due the end of the week, half a dozen planets all lined up for trouble. How much worse could you make things?"

"I'll tell you," Torrence answered. "I'm going to sell my trumpet and my car and I'm going to the dog races in Daytona Beach and I'm going to play every last dollar on a little bitch named Lullabell and come home rich or broke."

"When?" Beulah said, as if there was something she could do about Torrence's plan if she had enough time. Turned out it wasn't *her* time she was worried about, it was star time.

"Mercury in retrograde," she said, "bad for day-to-day travel, signing contracts, and betting on female greyhounds. Wait a while."

"No way in hell am I waiting," Torrence said, and he pushed his chair back and dropped his silverware and napkin to the floor as he charged out of the house.

Lyman stood up and started clearing the dishes with his good hand and June told me to come on back to our room, she had something she wanted to show me. She went right to the bureau and took a little white satin drawstring bag out of the top drawer. "I just love that Torrence," she said to me. "He's got the best outlook of any man I ever knew." She sat down on the bed and opened the bag. "Look here," she said, "it's all we got. Near to three hundred dollars and I'm going to give it to Torrence and tell him to put every last dollar on Lullabell. I'm tired of playing it safe too. I got to do something big."

I counted the money June let me take from the bag. It was exactly $295. I'd never much thought about money before, but now this roll of dollars was like an anchor in my hand, a way to fix us some place steady. "What if we lose it?" I asked.

"We'll be broke, just like Torrence. But see here, Lily, what we got isn't enough to make much of a difference anyway. On the other hand, what we might win could set us up in style. Get us a little cottage out by the beach. I've been thinking about Mardi Gras, a trip to New Orleans."

I didn't even want to go to New Orleans—Caroline had once told me that they buried their dead above ground, so their ghosts had no work at all to set themselves free, never mind that I didn't even believe in ghosts. But if June was going all the way to Louisiana, I wanted to go with her. I wanted to meet a Cajun and see the bayous and eat dirty rice like I'd read about in school. I wanted me and my mother to hear Dixieland jazz and wear beautiful masks and show our faces to each other alone. I wanted her to go to New Orleans and I wanted her to want me with her.

"I'm going too," I said.

"Mardi Gras's no place for you, Lily," is all she said.

The doorbell rang, and Beulah called out, "Lily, it's your Lucas."

The future looked so wretched—I'd either be penniless with June or rich without her. I reached for my jacket from the hook on the back of the door. June grabbed up the little satin purse. "Here, sweetheart," she said, "you take this and keep it somewhere, buy yourself something nice." She handed me a five-dollar bill, which I stuffed into my pocket, though what I wanted to do was spit on it and tear it up and throw it in her face, all of which my mother saw. "Say listen, you don't want it, you give it here, you give it right back to me."

"I hate your guts," I hissed, and ran down the hall to the living room, past Lucas, out the front door, and up the street with him somewhere behind me.

It was so cold out I could see my breath and I got a stitch in my side just as I was running past the little Baptist church about a mile from the house, which is where Lucas caught up with me. For maybe another mile or so, I ran with my hand to the stitch, and me and him kept perfect time. Finally, he stopped me. He was breathing hard through his mouth and his face was dripping with sweat. "That's enough," he said. "I could keep going but I don't even know why we're running and I'll be damned if I'll wear myself out for no good reason."

For a second I thought he was angry because of his words, but then he smiled and he kissed my forehead. His breath stirred up my hair and my scalp and my insides like warm fingers of a gentle hand. I fell against him and breathed his damp skin where the collar of his jacket was open. He put his arm around me and steered me a good distance, through a big gate and well past a trailer park where lights at a half-dozen trailer windows burned pale through the fine rain that had started to fall, and on to where he laid me down beside him, underneath a live oak.

We didn't say much, just listened to the rain. You could hear raccoons and skunks scratching around in the brush and every now and then, voices from the park. It was cold on the ground and I sat up and leaned against the thick tree trunk. Lucas sat up too and pulled a pack of cigarettes from his jacket pocket, lit one, took a drag, and spit a piece of tobacco from his mouth the way I'd seen Nate do a thousand times. I looked at the wrapper. They were not Pall Malls, his usual brand, they were Lucky Strikes, Nate's brand.

"LSMFT, Lucky Strike Means Fine Tobacco," I said.

"LSMFT, Loose Straps Means Floppy Titties," Lucas said.

"Now, that's something my father never mentioned," I said.

Lucas took a long drag and let the smoke trickle from his mouth. "I got news for you," he said when the smoke was all out of him. "Your father is something you never mention. It's like you didn't have one."

I stood up and brushed the dirt from my skirt and my legs. I could feel my lips curling and a lump in my throat big as a goiter. " 'Course I have a father," I said. "And I don't know what you're saying about I never mention him, because I know for a fact I talk about him all the time."

Lucas laughed like curling lips and goiters were a big joke. "Like when?" he said. "Just tell me one time you ever said anything to me about your father, or your mother, far as that goes. You never say much about her either."

Good God almighty, I was jumping now, and pounding the ground with each step, waving my arms and shaking my head like a real crazy person, like Caroline, like I was her or she was right there inside me. "You can just go fuck yourself, Lucas Holman, if you think I remember everything I ever said to you so I can say it back to you now."

"Christ sake, Lily," he said, "I don't know what it is makes you turn on me like that, like I'd done something wrong."

"You did do something wrong," I shrieked, "you got born."

Lucas looked at me real steady for a minute, steady but not deep—what was deepest inside him, he'd already taken from me. Then he stood up, dropped his cigarette in the dirt and ground it out with his heel, pulled his jacket closed and buttoned it at the collar, sunk his hands into his jacket pockets, and began to walk back toward the trailers and the road, no uncertainty in his gait, no asking at his back.

Like the rain was just waiting for a sign from Lucas, now it really let loose so the sheltering reach of the oak tree was no shelter at all. But I waited till I was sure he was well ahead of me before I left that place, and then I took my time, as I let the truth of Lucas's words seep in with the rain, memories of Nate slowing me down, memories of June too, and June and Nate together, and June when Nate was gone, and Nate always gone, and then us too, gone for always.

# Chapter 8

If I'd been looking, I bet I could have seen the seed of our leaving Sally and Neil Shriver's house in Welch, West Virginia, right from the start, but I tried not to mind how June was with her cousin's husband. And then, too, Sally was so glad to see us, warm and gracious, asked us no questions, as if our popping in from 120 miles away at six-thirty in the morning was nothing out of the ordinary. Never mind that June hadn't phoned or even sent a Christmas card in years, she put on her apron to make us some breakfast, corned beef hash from a can and poached eggs tough as a Goodyear, and sent us to get ourselves settled in their guest room.

"This was meant to be the baby's room," June said as we were unpacking our bags, "but they never had children." She shook the wrinkles from a pair of white trousers and laid them on one of the twin beds, reached for a cigarette from her pocket, packed the tobacco down with a couple of taps on the arm of a morris chair. "Of course, they never have guests either," she went on, the cigarette now lit and loose between her lips, "because Sally won't let anybody near Neil, male the same as female, like he's a god but only one person can worship him, her."

Sally kept a portrait-sized color photograph of Neil framed and mounted on the living room wall above the sofa and another one nearly that big in the kitchen over the table, so I had a chance to study him before he got home late that night from his job at a logging camp about twenty miles from Welch. He *was* a good-looking man, fair, with a thick head of hair turned prematurely gray and eyes an unholy color of blue. In person he smelled sweetly of sawdust, and he was taller than I'd imagined. His voice was big too, and deep, and I liked that his name started with an *N*, because so did Nate's, and both names had one syllable apiece. And if I was shy with him, and protective of the part of me my father still possessed and raw from being torn away, that didn't mean I wouldn't have given all I had for even a little of Neil's attention. But when Sally served him a plate of what we'd eaten earlier, overcooked meat loaf and dried-out macaroni and cheese, and we all sat with him while he had his meal, he wouldn't even look at me when he asked me to pass the salt and pepper.

Actually, it didn't take long to decide that I didn't much like him. Pretty as his eyes were, blue was not green, and he didn't so much look at you as through you, past you. He always had food between his teeth, and when he sang, he looked at June to let her know his songs were for her, pretending that Sally wasn't standing two feet away, drying the dishes or wiping the table, and him right up close to my mother, though he'd be sure to say, " 'Scuse me," as though there wasn't room for the two of them in a hall big enough to park a truck in.

You'd have thought Sally'd be the first to notice what was going on between June and Neil, but it took her a while, and in the meantime June got the job at the fabric store in town and I stayed home with Sally, walked in the woods, raked the garden, mowed the lawn, pulled the weeds from around the front and back stoop, read Sally's magazines, as I lay in the hammock on sunny days or sat at the kitchen table when it rained, while Sally practiced her guitar and dusted her bric-a-brac—she had a three-tiered table and a matching shelf crowded with over two hundred china figurines, rabbits, frogs, and turtles mostly. And when she asked if I wanted her to teach me a few chords, I said no, I was tired, or I had some ironing to do for June. Ironing, indeed, she said, why hadn't June put me in school or camp? Fall was soon enough, is what I told her, like June told me. Fall? Were we staying on that long? Because God knew she'd minded her own business for a good while, but now she had to know what on earth happened back there in Covington.

I thought I was telling her the truth when I said I didn't know, since June would never talk about it. "I'm finished with that part of my life, I've left it behind me once and for all," she'd insisted. "You come at me with your questions, I got news for you, talking about it's the same as living it all over again, and I'll be damned to hell if I'll do that."

The truth is I *had* figured some of it out myself. I knew it had to do with how Nate sending her home alone that night meant something more than just that, and it had to do with Caroline too, but even though June said she was a mad-woman, a danger to herself and others and better suited to the state asylum than life among civilized people, I had a different understanding of her. I knew that some of her ways were dangerous, but some were enchanting, like how she be-lieved in things you couldn't see, some of them deep, some of them righteous.

In Welch, I went back and forth about my grandmother as I did about most things, like about what was going on at the Shrivers'. Because maybe there wasn't anything for Sally to notice, since the truth was I'd never seen Neil and June kiss outright, I'd never seen them sneaking off someplace together or heard them make a coincidence of an unexpected meeting in town or out by the shed, the way you do when you've got something to hide. The way I did when one of them or Sally would come upon me hanging up the telephone after a useless call I'd made home to Covington: how I'd hoped and prayed that Nate would answer, I could almost hear his voice through the ringing on the line and feel the great relief of his smiling eyes as if they'd never grown dull to me at all. But it was always Caroline who said hello and instantly I was spooked by my own confusion as all my memories of her collapsed into one picture so she was flying out the attic window to dance naked in the moonlight with a deck of playing cards scattered at her feet and I always hung up.

"I didn't hear the phone ring," June would say, poking her head in the kitchen at just the right moment, like she was tuned in to me that way, radio waves, extrasensory perception.

"It was a wrong number," I'd explain.

Or Sally, seeing me with the phone in my hand, might ask if the party line was tied up and I'd say no, or I didn't know, I was just looking at the receiver. For what? she'd ask with a smile, like it was such a quaint idea, and her smile irked me so I wouldn't even answer. Of course if it was Neil, no matter how upset I was I didn't have to speak, something made easy by the fact that he never spoke to me.

And then it was precisely what he said one Saturday morning in early fall, not to me, but about me, that put an end to all my uncertainty, him and June an awkward heap on the floor amidst a brittle carpeting of Sally's broken figurines—bits of frogs' legs, turtle shells, and rabbit ears crunching and cracking under their weight, the three-tiered table turned on its side, one single wild hare hanging from a scalloped wooden edge by its chin—Sally in from the mailbox at the far end of their hundred-foot drive now come upon them, me too, out from the bedroom for the racket alone.

"Goddamn it, I told you that girl was trouble," Neil said, brushing china dust from his knees with one hand, pointing at me with the other. "And now look at the ruin she's made of your treasures," paying no mind to the grotesque smear June's lipstick had made of his mouth, or her blouse open so her white lace slip showed clear down to her waist.

Sally turned from the living room toward the kitchen, came back only a few seconds later with the broom and the dustpan, handed them both to Neil. "You better get busy," she said to him, squinting and showing her dog teeth, "and you two just better git," she said to me and June.

My mother was jittery and I was hopelessly underfoot, needing to be near her as we packed our bags and loaded up the car, ashamed of the need and her ornery impatience with me when I asked questions to which I knew the answers.

We would have been on our way before noon, but I couldn't find the Robin Hood watch Caroline had brought me from Pennsylvania, maybe I'd lost it in the woods. June searched my face and then, I suspect because of what she saw there, she said okay, we could take a quick look, even though the damned thing wasn't worth the time it would take to find it. We crossed a neighbor's wide field of blackened hay stubble, then low bushes and ferns, stiff and dry, that scratched our bare legs, and all along the way our eyes tracked the path, but we didn't find the watch. June said it was just as well, the more of Caroline and home we left behind us, the better off we'd be.

We'd begun our walk back to the car when she said she had something in her shoe. We stopped beside a shallow stream and sat on a big rock and she dug a pebble from one of her flats. A dull midmorning sun turned the yellow poplar leaves waxen as she dipped her bare feet in the cool water. Hadn't we better get going? I asked her, as afraid of staying as I was of leaving. June said another five minutes wouldn't make any difference to anyone and she unlaced my shoes and rolled off my socks and trickled water on my toes. If we followed that stream, she said, we'd see how it made its way toward some wide river, which was she didn't know how many miles away, but you could be sure that there was one, because water was always drawn to water. Then she stroked my neck with a slip of timothy and told me a story about a boy she'd had a crush on named Troy, he was a sailor out of Newport News and they'd met at a bar nearby, where the windows looked out on the James River making its way to the Chesapeake Bay and the boy had said it was just like him making his way to June.

And she told me once again, because I'd heard this story before, how she and Nate had met—it was at a dance in Virginia Beach, and the band was playing a feeble version of "Do Nothing Till You Hear from Me," the trumpets straining for every note, when suddenly she'd seen this tall, slim boy walking toward her, gliding really, because that was the way he moved. And then, as if the band knew he deserved a song that better suited his step, they started "Sentimental Journey." He'd whirled her around that dance floor, it was like a fairy tale, he smelled like a pirate, velvety, golden, ruffled.

After she finished, I said, "I already heard that part. What about the other?"

"I don't know what you mean," she said.

"Well, that was the beginning," I said. "I never heard the end."

She pulled up a handful of weeds and twisted them into a rope. She looked toward the woods where a jaybird was chattering, and then she looked at me and then she looked toward the jay again. "There's not much to tell," she said. "That woman, the one he was with at the motel in Radford, she was there at the Greenbriar. She walked right up to our table like it was all planned, which I guess it was, and she said she had her car waiting outside. She said she'd still keep what she called their deal, she'd set him up in business for himself, all he had to do was walk out of that place with her right then and there. And that's just what he did."

"Did he say he was sorry?"

"Uh-huh."

"Did he say he loved you? Did he say he loved me?"

June didn't answer. She flicked her fingers at the gnats that buzzed around her head and dug her toes in among the pebbles at the bottom of the stream. I splashed the water with my feet so it splattered all over me and her and I yelled as loud as I could, "I know you just made that whole shit-heeled thing up." I picked up a handful of pebbles and I threw them close enough so she said if I picked up another I'd better be ready to eat it. I picked up one single pebble and I threw it across the stream and I said, "I know why you like to make up such ugly things, it's because you're so ugly."

"Look who's talking," June said. She took her feet out of the water, dried them on her skirt, put her shoes on, and stood up. "It's getting late," she said, then she set off like she knew where she was going. I was in no hurry to join her. Now I threw pebbles in earnest, growled dirty words, hated everybody I knew, and named and damned them out loud, damned my father loudest of them all.

I don't know how far she went or how long she was gone, but I was finally about ready to follow her back to the car when she reappeared. "Christ sake, Lily," she said with her hands on her hips and her mouth twisted mean and cross, "I'm lost."

I looked around at the stream and the woods and the fallen trees still echoing with my curses. I knew where we were and I told her so, though I wished I was willing to stay there forever, just for the sake of making her do the same. She looked at me with perfect scorn and said she doubted I could find our way. "I can too," I insisted, glad for the challenge. "I've been here before."

She looked around like the trees themselves might tell her what business I'd had in the place. "When?" she asked.

"A couple of times," I said, and then I hesitated, because there was some things I wanted her to know about and there was some I liked to keep to myself. "I used to come out here," I explained, "with Alice."

"With Alice? Sally's cat? What on earth are you talking about?"

The truth was I'd never meant to speak a word to June about my times in the woods with Sally and Neil's old calico, but she wouldn't leave me alone and something about what had happened with the cat went just right with the way I was feeling. So I told her—how I always thought Alice wasn't much good for anything, didn't run after mice or the moles that ate Sally's garden, didn't care to have you pet her, didn't purr and stretch pretty in the sun the way some cats do. All she did was sleep on a ratty old chair and pee on the honeysuckle by the door. And worst of all, when she opened her mouth to cry or whine, she only made a scratchy sound, like she had something caught in her throat.

When I was in the house alone with her she used to come up on me. I'd pretend I didn't notice her, but she wouldn't have it. If I was sitting on the sofa and reading a magazine, she'd start clawing the skirt of the slipcover. If I was ironing a blouse, she'd knead my shoe. At first I'd just say "Shoo!" but she wouldn't mind, so I'd give her a swat.

"What do you mean, a swat?" June said.

"Usually I'd hit her with the back of my hand, but once when I was out here in the woods, down on my knees drawing in the dirt with a rock, she came right up to me. She opened her mouth and let that awful sound loose on me. 'Scat,' I hollered at her, but she stood there, like she was daring me to hit her with that rock. So I did. I hit her plenty hard, and she gave a horrible cry and made her face all screwed up like it was caving in on itself and then she ran away. Another time I held her down with my one hand spread across her back, pushing her stomach to the ground like this," and I showed June, making my palm and my fingers flat to the bank of the stream.

"You did not either," June said.

"Yes I did," I said, and I could feel my voice grow stronger and a rush of blood heat up my cheeks. "And you know, it took some thinking ahead," I taunted. "I had to make sure I hit her hard enough so I enjoyed it, but not so hard that she looked like she'd been messed with. I didn't want her limping around the house so Sally would say, 'Look at Alice. I wonder what's the matter with her?' I knew if she made a fuss over that cat I'd have a fit."

June had her eyes locked in a stare on I didn't know what, and when she spoke, her voice sounded like it was locked in that stare too. "Goddamn it, Lily," she said, "did you kill her?"

"No, I didn't," which was the absolute truth, she'd died of old age.

"But you must have been glad when she went."

"I expected I would be, but I wasn't. I thought about her all the time, and I hated her just as much dead as I'd hated her when she was alive."

June chipped at her fingernail polish with a twig, she made confetti out of a maple leaf. Then she said, "Christ sake, I wish you hadn't told me a word of it."

"You asked me," I said, even though all the while I could see I was shocking her, and I liked it. But then she started to cry and I remembered how she'd cried the day we left Covington so at first I wondered if it was just a matter of our leaving, but then I knew it wasn't, because there was more than tears. She began to shake her head and sob, saying my name again and again. It made me know how sad I was, so I started crying too. When I could I said, "I'm sorry, Mama," and when she said, "What are you sorry for?" I answered, "Everything."

# Chapter 9

Lullabell did not win the seventh race the next day, she didn't even place or show, and Torrence was busted and bitter. It took him until late that night to get home—he'd sold his car just like he'd promised, so he had to hitchhike from Daytona in the rain. He had to stop at bars and roadhouses along the way and play cards and snooker for beers and shots of whiskey and when he walked into the house, slamming doors behind him so the walls shook, kicking at throw rugs and footstools, Beulah set up a wail.

It was my thirteenth birthday, and I'd been waiting for somebody to make something of it, but now I could hear Torrence and June hollering in the back of the house where he'd found her waiting, June's voice louder than his, angrier too, but then somebody laughed, I think it was Torrence, then June was laughing too, and he started singing "Camptown ladies sing this song, doo-dah, doo-dah," and soon the two of them were coming down the hall, singing and laughing still and I knew that there wasn't going to be any birthday anything. They stopped on their way out the back door just long enough for June to drop the empty white satin bag at my feet and then they left in the Buick with the radio blasting.

For two days and two nights I waited at the kitchen table for my mother to come home, and when I wasn't waiting for her, I was waiting for Lucas and I didn't care about my birthday anymore, I didn't care if I never had a birthday again, just so long as I didn't have to be alone. But alone I was and I found that three days without either one of them was more than I could stand, especially with Beulah ragging on Lyman every time she left her room to pee or drink a glass of water and Lyman pulling at his eyebrows and chewing his fingernails to the quick.

On the third day I went to meet Charlene after school and ask if I could go home with her. She looked frightened at first, but then she said yes, she was sure it would be okay, so long as I didn't mind sharing her supper and sleeping with her too. Her bed was a cot, she explained, but she'd let me have the pillow and she had an almost new baby-doll nightgown she'd let me wear.

Charlene's clapboard house was set among a bunch of little houses at the edge of a cypress swamp, just two rooms and a screened-in porch with lots of holes in the screening. Her mother was a small woman with Charlene's pretty face and fair skin, which I guessed she'd protected from years in the sun with the big-brimmed hat that hung by the door. But she had a pot belly and a limp from what years of squatting among rows of dirt crops had done to her hips. Charlene's father was small too, but wiry where her mother was slack, and dark-skinned from years of working with the sun on his face. They told me to call them by their first names, Hilda and Morton, and they said I was welcome, and at first it seemed like that was about all they were going to say.

It was a quiet house, no radio or TV and no singing,

mostly hushed voices where Hilda and Morton spoke to each other in the kitchen, which was also their bedroom, or where Hilda spoke to Charlene behind the closed bathroom door. Suppertime that first night was quiet too, but on the second night—seems like they needed to get used to having me among them—when the dishes were washed and put away, Hilda boiled ground chicory in a pot so the room filled with sweet steam and Morton smoked his pipe, and me and Charlene sat and listened to her parents' stories about the years they'd lived in Texas—cattle thieves, shrimp boats, beautiful Mexican women, oil rigs, ten-gallon hats.

On the third night, Hilda told me how they'd come east to Florida with baby Charlene and big dreams that never came true, but how just the same, they thanked God every day for what they'd got. "We could feel sorry for ourselves," Hilda said, "but we seen what other folks was dealt."

I looked at Charlene like she might explain what her mother meant, but she was picking at the chipped cup in her hands. So I asked Hilda directly what they had seen.

"Saw a woman die from a snakebite and another die of heatstroke, and it's surprising how much dying of the one looks like dying of the other," Hilda said. "Saw a child throw himself into the river after his daddy drowned there, and I said to myself there's no new way of dying, boy dying just like his pap. Then I saw something new, my own brother hit by lightning, him and his lawn chair jumped three feet off the ground, the chair carried to the uppermost branches of a banyan tree by the wind, and that boy flat on his face with his fingernails black and his hair singed and a horrible smell about him from the frying and the load the lightning set loose in his pants."

I wanted to say something, but I couldn't get my mouth to work. "Take it easy there, Hilda," Morton said through the pipestem clenched between his teeth. "You don't want to give Lily nightmares."

Hilda reached across the table and rubbed my hand. "Didn't mean to scare you none," she said, and she took the chicory from the stovetop and poured what was left in the pot into my cup.

That night I couldn't sleep. Even though it was warm they kept the kerosene heater on and the smell of it turned my stomach. I could feel the termites eating at the wood behind my back where I sat against the wall at the foot of Charlene's cot, thinking about snakebites and heatstroke and lightning. I'd read in the papers about such things happening to people I didn't know, but nothing so dreadful had ever happened to me or my family. I wished I was with June someplace safe and I made up my mind to leave that house and never return, because what if it rubbed off on me, their suffering and hard times?

Right at dawn Charlene woke up and came to sit beside me with her head in my lap and her eyes searching mine. I brushed her fine yellow hair from her forehead. "You're going home soon, aren't you?" she said.

"This very morning," I answered her.

There was just our Buick parked in the muddy driveway beside the Youngers' garage, and as soon as I stepped inside the house, I got a feeling that I'd made a horrible mistake, this was no safe place at all. It didn't make me feel safe that the kitchen table was bare and there was no dirty dishes in the sink and none drying in the drainer on the counter. All the cushions set right on the chairs and the sofa in the living room didn't make me feel safe either, nor did the open door of Beulah's bedroom, her bed made, and in the bathroom every towel dry and hanging neatly from the hooks on the back of the door. But by the time I walked into the back bedroom, the one I shared with June, I was prepared for the things I saw: our bed stripped of linens, the spread folded carefully over the footboard, our suitcases and duffel bags packed and piled by the door.

Just the same, I felt like something had a hold of my chest so I could barely draw a breath. I was set to run, but I couldn't think where to run to. Then I saw my reflection in the mirror above the bureau and I gave myself a horrible fright—my face was drawn and my hair was a nest of knots and my clothes were miserably soiled from nearly a week of wear. But what I saw in the mirror didn't frighten me half so much as what I saw beside it.

You have to wonder about the way your mind works, how it chooses for your eyes, from all the things before you, what you see *first*—stripped bed, packed bags, and you looking back at yourself in the mirror—and what you see *later*—June standing in the corner, a far worse sight than me: her blond hair caked with mud; on her cheek a red and angry scab already forming over a scrape the size of a fried egg; her white blouse torn at the collar, the buttons hanging off the front like loose teeth; her hand clutching the waist of her filthy white sharkskin skirt; her legs bruised and bloody, her feet bare, her toes curled tight as salted snails.

When she spoke her voice sounded like ripping sheets for rags. "Don't come near me," she said.

I could feel my head shaking, saying a hundred little no's every second—no, I wouldn't go near her, no, I couldn't stay away, no, it hadn't happened, like I was saying no to the truth before I even knew what it was.

I swallowed hard and I made my voice as quiet as hers. "What do you want me to do?" I asked. It seemed like she was thinking about it too, trying to figure out what was next. And maybe that *is* what she was thinking at first, but then the telephone rang—I jumped when I heard it, but June didn't move—and some more time passed and I heard the postman drop the mail into the box at the front door. My feet were pins and needles and I had a crick in my neck, I was tired and cold and I felt like I had to pee. Then I remembered that I hadn't had anything to drink that morning so I probably didn't have to pee. June cleared her throat a couple of times, and once I think she spoke, though I couldn't make her out, her lips hardly moved.

I don't know what time it was I lay down on the bed, slowly, and pulled the spread over myself and closed my eyes. I fell asleep, and I guess I was still sleeping when the noon whistle blew and I felt June's weight on the mattress. She lifted the spread and lay down behind me. Her clothes and skin were cool against my back and her fingers gripped mine so tight I cried out. "Shhhhh," she whispered, and then she told me what had happened.

The night they left, her and Torrence had made it as far south as Delray Beach before the gas gave out. Torrence said that since they weren't going any place in particular, Delray Beach was as good a place as any to stop. They took a room at a little motel on A1A. The lady at the office wanted him to pay in advance, but Torrence made up some story about his wife having the money in her purse but she was sick with some kind of woman's ailment so he didn't want to bother her, seemed like a hot bath was what she needed, did they have a room with a tub and could he please bring the lady the money in the morning.

"They had a tub all right," June muttered in my ear. "Filthiest goddamned thing I ever saw. Wouldn't wash the dog in it."

I thought her swearing was a sign that her strength was coming back and I made to turn around so we could be face to face, but she tightened her grip and held me as I lay. "You weren't sick anyway, were you?" I asked her just the same because I wasn't going to pass up the chance to keep this bit of liveliness going.

"Wasn't sick," she said, her voice dull again, her grip gone limp, "but I was drunk. And I stayed drunk for the next five days. Torrence kept going out for a couple of hours, leaving me to read the magazines and dimestore novels he'd brought me the last time he'd gone out, and every time he came back he'd have a pint of bourbon or whiskey with him."

"Where was he getting the money?"

"Beats me," she said. "Some hustle, I guess. He's got plenty of them, poker, pool, I've seen him hustle a man for the weather." She turned to lie on her back. I rolled over beside her and watched the dust in a shaft of sunlight streaming in the window.

"Didn't you go out places?" I asked her. No, she said, she'd never left the room. He put the DO NOT DISTURB sign on their door and he brought her sandwiches and cigarettes and booze. Soon it got to where, with the drapes closed, she didn't even know when it was day or night, and drunk as she was she didn't really care. But five days of it was as much as she could take.

It was three o'clock in the morning—"Which morning?" I asked her. "Today," she said, "this very day"—when she got herself up from that bed and opened the door to their room, just as a man and a woman were going into a room a couple of doors down. She asked them the time, she asked them the day too, and when she realized it was the best part of a week since she and Torrence had left Vero Beach she sobered up real fast.

She scoured that bathtub with some cleanser she found in the cupboard under the sink, she was so dirty she'd had half a mind to use the cleanser on herself, "All that alcohol," she said, "and the cigarettes, and the sex," and she sniffled as if her nose was stuffed up, but it wasn't. Then, like she wanted to make sure she answered my questions before I could ask them she said, "Not that I remember it, the sex, I mean. I just remember Torrence's face red and the stubble of his beard longer each time I looked at him above me, and his teeth yellow, I'd never noticed before how yellow his teeth were. Sometimes we were laughing while we were doing it. A couple of times I was out cold and I came to from him, from him inside me."

Now I was sure I had to pee. In fact, I really needed some air, but June kept right on talking, raised her voice when I got up from the bed and followed me to the bathroom, stood right there with her foot jammed between the door and the frame while I sat on the toilet. Then she trailed me into the kitchen, hovered too close beside me at the sink, and took my glass of water from my hand before I was through. God, she swallowed fast, nearly choked, but still she kept on with her story while I was spreading mayonnaise on a half-dozen slices of stale bread.

She couldn't much remember the sex, but she could smell it. She filled the tub with water so hot the room clouded up with steam, and she scrubbed herself again and again and washed her hair with the bar soap and rinsed it under the running tap and then she let the water out of the tub and filled it again and soaked till the hot water cooled.

After the bath came the hardest part, putting the same clothes on, but she tucked her shirt into her skirt and gave it a good yank, wiped the mud from her shoes with the corner of a washcloth, and sat down to wait for Torrence to get back so she could come home. "I didn't have to wait very long," she said, taking a slice of bread from the plate I'd set between us on the kitchen table. "But he didn't want to leave. He wanted us to stay right there, because he was doing some kind of business with a guy from a fishing boat in Boynton

Beach and there was a few hundred dollars in it for us, but we had to stick around for another couple of days." She nibbled at the bread. I folded the last slice in half, then in half again, and shoved it into my mouth, chewed on it till it turned to a rubbery lump, swallowed it whole.

" 'I can't stay here. I got to get home and see about Lily. I've been gone too long.' That's what I told him," June said, "but he said forget it, he'd worked too hard to get something going, he wasn't going to blow it now. And how come I all of a sudden got it in my head that I had to be a mother, because if it was so damned important, why hadn't I bothered about it for the last five days. Which really pissed me off, so I told him to go fuck himself, and that's when he hit me."

I already knew there wasn't any bread left and the bananas in the basket on the counter were rotten and the milk was probably spoiled, so I poured some salt from the saltshaker onto the table and I stuck the grains to my fingertip one at a time and let the salt melt on my tongue. June watched for a bit like I was doing it for show, but then she grabbed the shaker and brushed the salt from the tabletop onto the floor. "Don't do that," she said. "Salt makes you hold your water."

"Did you hit him back?" I asked, praying to God that she had, even though I was sitting right in front of the evidence that if she had, it had cost her plenty.

"I did at first," she answered, "but he was a lot stronger than me, and to tell you the truth, I believe that if I'd kept my hands to myself it might have gone easier for me. As it is, I think I got off cheap." She brushed her cheek like she could brush away the nasty wound there. "The worst of it was him chasing me out to the parking lot and dragging me back inside the room and the sex that came after, but even that wasn't a whole lot worse than what had already happened a dozen times or more. And the truth is he finally passed out and I could get away. It's all over now. I guess that's what really matters."

I was asking God to please let her stop talking, begging Him to get her to change the subject or decide it wasn't that important, when the telephone rang. "I'll get it," I said.

"Let it ring, Lily," June said, and she held my wrist and dug her fingernails into my flesh and I cried out but she didn't flinch.

"It might be Beulah or Lyman," I said.

"I don't care who it is," June said. "And anyway, Lyman's dead and Beulah's gone to Gainesville."

It wouldn't take me more than a half hour to walk back to Charlene's. A couple of times I'd gone with her to a store not far from her house run by a lady who had a fox terrier named Jim. I bet she'd let me wait with her until Charlene and Hilda and Morton got home, and I knew the Sipps would have me back.

The telephone was still ringing, but I heard it now as if it was a new call and I made to get up to answer it like I hadn't already tried before and this time June let me go. The line was dead by the time I picked up the receiver, but at least I wasn't in the same room with my mother anymore. I was standing in the hall between the living room and the kitchen, and my back was turned to her so it was almost like she wasn't there. I dialed the operator and gave her my name and our telephone number in Covington and said I'd speak collect to anybody that answered. June-who-wasn't-there snickered loud in the kitchen, "Oh, Lily," she said as the telephone line rang and rang, "goddamn it, Lily," she said as the line clicked and Caroline said hello. I could hear June's chair scraping the kitchen floor while the operator spoke my name and asked my grandmother if she'd pay for the call, and then my mother was right there before me when the line went dead and the operator said, "I'm sorry, would you like me to place your call again?" I handed the receiver to June. I could hear the operator say, "Ma'am?" as my mother hung up the phone.

We were nearly the same height now, me and June, and it seemed, as we stood there in the shadowy hall, like we were a good match that way. Our breathing was a good match too, I could see her chest rise and fall with mine, fast at first, then slower, and slower still, and all the things I was feeling seemed to drain from me like sand from a fist.

"I'm it," she said.

"What do you mean?"

"I'm all you got."

Suddenly she looked short, shorter than me, and young, like a girl, and I knew it and I said it at the same time. "I'm all you got too."

She nodded her head and wiped her nose with the back of her hand. "I know," she said. "Well, it's not the end of the world," she added.

The end of the world? I wondered. Then I remembered. "Charlene's mother knew somebody died of a snakebite and somebody else who died of heatstroke," I said.

"Lyman got himself hit by a car," June said. "Walked right in front of a 1953 Mercury doing sixty-five miles an hour out on Blue Cypress Lake Road."

"She knew a father and son both drowned in the same river," I said.

"I saw Beulah when I got back here this morning," June said. "She was loading her things into the back of an old junk car. She never introduced me to the driver. She told me about Lyman and she said she'd packed our bags and hoped we'd be gone when she comes back from Gainesville."

"She saw her own brother hit by lightning," I said. "Turned his fingernails black and singed his hair and loosed his bowels."

"Look," she said, and she dug into the pocket of her skirt and pulled out a little bar of soap wrapped in waxy orange paper. "I brought this for you. It's for your birthday." I took the soap from her hand and sniffed it. It smelled like orange blossoms and it made my eyes tear with gratitude and regret. "Let's you and me clean ourselves up and put everything in the car and get the hell out of here," June said. "And Lily, don't ask me where we're going. We got near to a full tank of gas, courtesy of Torrence Younger . . ."

"And I still got the five dollars you gave me," I cut in.

"Okay," she said. "Well then, 'Bye, Bye, Blackbird.' "

"What's that?" I asked.

"It's a song," she said.

"I remember that song. How does it go?"

" 'Pack up all my cares and woe, here I go singing low . . .' "

# Chapter 10

At least she wanted me with her, that's how I consoled myself, at least she wasn't going off without me. Just the same, as we drove away from Vero Beach, headed west on Route 60, I felt like I had a cold in my skin and everything that touched me hurt. It was as if it was me Torrence Younger had beat up in that room, even Beulah's home better than no home, now it was two places we'd been asked to leave, suddenly the world was shrinking around us and the smaller it got the less room there was for us in it.

That first day, June said I looked peaked and had me drink tea, which she made from a jar of molasses we took from Beulah's cupboard and cups of hot water she ordered at every place that looked like we could get one for free if we paid for something else, a doughnut, a plate of grits. I guess she was feeling frail herself because her hand shook each time she gave me the cup. One time I took her hand with the cup so we were both holding the tea to my lips, tempting each other with the comfort we wanted to share, the comfort we needed, and in some unspoken way I think we each yielded to that temptation and that need, for how our two hands steadied each other, the tea a soothing vapor between us. "Sip," she said softly, and then we both swallowed.

June drove slower than I'd ever known her to go. Sometimes she'd stop the car by the side of the road and we'd look out the window at some bird or a cropduster sweeping across newly sown fields. We didn't put on the radio or talk, and we didn't bother with a map, I guess because we didn't know where we were going. So it's no surprise that after a lot of weaving and wandering we wound up the very next day right back on Route 60 headed east.

"What'd that sign say?" she asked, just after we passed the turn-off for Lake Kissimmee. "Did that sign say what I think it said?"

"Said Vero Beach seventy-three miles." June pulled over. We looked at each other for a minute, then at the sweep of Florida that surrounded us, land spread wide and flat, the sky tirelessly blue except to the west, where tall white clouds bumped around in a slow race to nowhere.

"Maybe you better get the map," she said. We laid it out on the steering wheel and located ourselves at the junction of Route 17, and sure enough, due east, there was Vero Beach. "Well, at least we're not lost," June said with a small but complicated little laugh.

"At least we know where we're going," I said, my laugh fuller and simpler for the solace it gave me, the great relief.

"Even if we don't want to go there," June added, her laugh, even her smile gone now.

"We *could* go back just for the night," I said, half joking, half not, "sleep in our old bed. We could stop at Charlene's and I could tell her good-bye, I could say good-bye to Lucas."

"Now there's an idea," she said, her smile back, cruel. "Maybe we could have supper with Torrence, see how he's doing."

She turned the car around so we were headed west again and we rode on a few miles. We slept that night in the Buick like we had the night before. We parked at a rest stop and sat on the hood of the car and ate the last of the sardines and crackers we'd taken from Beulah's. Then June leaned back against the windshield and dozed off and I stared out into the pine forest of the loneliest place I'd ever been. When the mosquitoes started to get to me, I woke her and we climbed into the car and rolled up the windows.

She lay down in the back and I sat in the front behind the wheel. I thought it would be better if I didn't sleep, because I had a lot of things on my mind, that's what I thought. But the din of the cicadas ruined my concentration and then a car pulled up alongside of us and the boy and the girl inside the car had their windows rolled down with no mind to the mosquitoes. I could hear them talking and carrying on and what I couldn't hear I could imagine, which was a big mistake, because my imagination turned to memory and the things I wished were memory, all of it beating so heavy on me I hardly felt my own touch until I was through.

Me and the boy and girl must have finished at about the same time—I was sitting there at the wheel of my mother's Buick in a muffled fit when I heard the girl giggling, I was still breathing heavy through my mouth, and when the boy started up their car and turned on the headlights June woke suddenly.

"What's that?" she asked.

"It's nothing. Go back to sleep," I said.

"Come back here with me," she said.

"There's not enough room," I said.

"I'm scared," she said.

"I'm right here," I said.

"Good. Good." She took a deep breath. "Long as I got you I know I'm doing the right thing. Long as we're together, I know everything's going to be all right. You and me, right, Lily?"

I took a deep breath too. "You and me," I said.

She clutched the back of my seat. "Lily?" she said.

Soon after that, she fell back to sleep. I nodded off now and then too, and when I wasn't sleeping, I was running my hand over the grip bumps on the steering wheel, counting them again and again, tugging at loose threads in the seams of the upholstery, thinking about our lives in Vero Beach and Welch and Covington, thinking about Caroline and her garden and her transistor radio and the sound of the dead telephone line, about Nate and his golf clubs and the woman from Radford and the church music at the motel and the pond on a moonlit night. I was remembering June and me on that road from Virginia to West Virginia and the jar of honey that shattered when my mother dropped it on the floor of the car, a puddle of it spreading slowly across the mat, like our lives and all the things that used to hold them shattered and spreading to I didn't know where.

Once again I put my hand between my legs and rubbed myself till my fingers ached and then I switched hands and I rubbed some more. Morning came gray and still and this time when my mother called my name I climbed over the seat and slept beside her until the sun broke through the clouds.

We were on the road by seven, that was what the clock said where we stopped at a filling station to wash our faces. And it was still early when we got to the outskirts of St. Petersberg with only some change in June's purse and a near-empty gas tank. She parked the car in front of a seedy-looking grocery store, combed her hair to make some of it hide the scab on her cheek, smoothed out her eyebrows with a little spit, went inside and came out twenty minutes later with a job at the checkout—minimum wage, an atrocious orange-and-yellow smock and an orange cap to match, the other checkout girls rude to June, rude to me too when I went inside to sit with her on her lunch break.

"You got to feel bad for them," June said, sounding like she didn't, as she ate another cocktail marshmallow from the bag in her lap. "They're poor and uneducated," she added, studying the label on the cellophane wrapper.

"I don't know if we're uneducated," I said, picking raisins from a red box, "but I know we're poor."

"Yeah, but we weren't meant to be," she said.

At the end of the work day, the store manager gave June an advance for her hours so we could get ourselves a room. "Oooo-eee," she whooped with wild extravagance, "fancy that man thinking I wanted his job for real." I whooped too, but I wasn't feeling extravagant, not one bit, because why couldn't she keep the job and why didn't we get us a room and why, why, why on earth were things such a goddamned horrible mess?

We slept in the car again that night, June in the front seat and me in the back, and when we woke up well into the morning, hot and sweaty, she was cooking. "Ransom Ryan Hood, that was his name, he was from Richmond and he inherited his daddy's wholesale food business and moved to Florida when I was pregnant with you."

"What of it?" I said, feeling cooked myself, rolling down the windows.

"Those tiny marshmallows I was eating at the grocery yesterday, they were Hood's, that's what the package said, Hood's Little Elegants." She tilted the rearview mirror so she could see herself the way she wanted to, without the shadow of Torrence's hand on her face, and then she grinned. "I knew that name rang a bell. And he liked me, he liked me enough to tell me so at a Kiwanis Club dance, with Nate as close to where we were standing as you are to me now." She straightened the mirror and started up the car.

"Where are we going?" I said, wiping my oily nose and forehead with a paper napkin from a pile of them on the seat beside me.

"Grocery shopping," she said.

We didn't go back to the store where she'd worked the day before, we went to another one that had cocktail marshmallows but not Hood's. June made a big fuss to the manager, like she was Mrs. John Jacob Astor and the failure of this market to carry the item she wanted was a personal affront and all the while the manager just stared at her wrinkled clothes and the scab on her face and sucked at his teeth. When June ran out of steam he suggested she try a market nearby, which we did, and they didn't have Little Elegants either. But the one after that did, and there was a Tampa address on the back of the package, which June wrote down on a piece of paper before she put the bag back on the shelf.

"Don't you want to buy them?" I said.

"What for?" she said.

"Well, for good luck or something," I said.

"The luck's finding them," she said. "The luck's what they're leading us to."

It didn't even take us an hour to drive to Tampa, but I didn't need very long to make trouble, not between us, all of it inside me, worry: what were grocery stores and addresses when practically overnight Vero Beach was already hazy in my memory, Welch and Covington like dreams you can't remember but they haunt you just the same, St. Petersburg and Tampa—what were they? Makebelieve places, holes in the earth that would swallow us up.

Finding the address we had for Hood's was no small task, and then when we finally located it out by the airport, the place was all boarded up. We went next door where there was a storm-door company, they made windows and skylights too. When I asked the man we spoke to what skylights were, June told me to shut up, it didn't matter, what mattered was did anybody know what had become of Hood's. The man said they'd always had a second place but the marshmallow business was slow so they'd given up the one next door and moved their whole operation to their other plant, and he gave her an address which turned out to be on the far side of town. We got lost a half-dozen times looking for it, and half-way through the half dozen, I said I was hungry—of course I was hungry, it was nearly three o'clock and we hadn't eaten a thing all day—and June said too bad and I thought to myself that worry was not trouble, starving to death, that was trouble.

It was nearly dark by the time we found the place and it was closed, but there was the sign, HOOD'S BEST in flashing red neon, and there was another sign, painted, that gave the names of their products—besides the Little Elegants, they made regular marshmallows and marshmallow fluff, as well as a line of products for bakers—confectioners' sugar, stabilizers, and artificial flavors. June turned the car off and sighed heavily.

"What are we going to do now?" I said.

"We're going to sit right here until this place opens in the morning, and then we're going to march ourselves right in to Ransom Ryan Hood's office and say, 'How do you do,' and then he's going to take care of us, we got nothing to worry about."

"What about tonight? Aren't we going to eat anything?" I said, so hungry I was nearly past hunger. "Aren't we going to get a room someplace so we can clean up?"

June looked at her fingernails as though they were the one sure way to tell if she needed cleaning up or not, and I guess between the chipped polish on top and the filth underneath, she decided maybe I had a point. She patted my head like you would a three-year-old and said she was glad she kept me around.

We had to drive a ways before we found a place to eat that didn't look either too fancy or too crummy, but it wasn't until we were sitting at the counter looking at the menus set before us by a dark-haired man in a grease-stained white shirt that we realized there was something peculiar about the place. "What the hell," June whispered and pointed to the flimsy paper she held, "I don't think this is English writing."

"Do you mean it's a foreign language?" I asked. "Like French?"

"French or maybe Italian," she said. "We better look for something else. I like to know what I'm eating."

We found a place a couple of doors down. June said it didn't seem likely there'd be two foreign places that close so we went in and of course the menu was in that language, except it was also in English, only they weren't serving hardly anything we'd heard of but chicken with rice. That's what we had, one order between us, and it came with slices of fried bananas so sweet they made your teeth ache, not that I complained, because I didn't, I was too happy to be eating. And the food made me feel more kindly toward June, so when she wiped my mouth with her napkin I wiped her mouth too, and then we smiled big like we were just recollecting how much we enjoyed each other, like the food had sharpened our memory.

After we finished, we looked around at the people sitting at the other tables and they were all dark-haired and dark-skinned and they were speaking "Spanish," that's what the girl said when she took our plates and offered us dessert,

"they're speaking Spanish," she said with a thick accent un-
like anything I'd ever heard. "You must be new to Ybor City.
That's where you are, Little Havana."

"You mean like Havana, Cuba?" June said.

"That's right," the girl said. "Did you ever hear of *café con
leche*?" She grinned. "Of course you never heard of it. It's
Cuban coffee. I'm going to bring you some and a dish of flan
too. You're going to like it."

The girl went off then and June began to make a more
careful survey of the room, scrutinizing the families and the
couples sitting at tables covered with what was left of big
meals. There was loud music playing from a speaker mounted
above the door to the kitchen, men's voices and a lot of
horns, and one of the couples at a table near us was holding
hands and singing along. "Spics," June said, "that's what
they are in here."

"What's spics?" I said.

"People from South America," she said.

"You mean Cubans?" I said.

"Cubans, Puerto Ricans, Venezuelans, all of them, they're
all spics." She lit a cigarette and blew out the match with far
more gusto than the little flame required. "And they're a
sleazy bunch. We got to get the hell out of here." I didn't say
anything, I especially didn't say the thing that was so obvious
to me, and I guess it was obvious to June too because when a
light-haired man dressed in a handsome black suit passed by
our table and dropped a set of keys on the floor, June
snatched them up before the man even had a chance to see
where they'd fallen, and when she handed them to him and
said, *"Señor,"* you'd have thought Spanish was all she knew,
when what she knew was that we were practically in a foreign
country, it was after dark, we had no place to stay, and no
one to guide us.

The man took his keys from June with a bow like I'd only seen in the movies and she smiled coyly and lowered her eyes. Then came this whole big to-do about her honor and his graciousness and my charm and more coffee and more flan and our bill and his billfold and when we'd all been about as delightful to one another as we could possibly be, he asked us to please forgive him, I think he said he had an engagement, but before he left was there anything he could do to assist us, a hotel? Yes, there was one quite nearby, a very reputable place, clean and modestly priced, would we be so kind as to take his business card so that the proprietor might know he sent us? and then he was gone.

June looked at his card and said his name out loud but I didn't catch it, I just heard, "All that blond hair, I didn't think he was a spic." Then she looked up and she smiled at me. "Don't I take good care of us?" I didn't say anything, I was busy feeling the Spanish man gone too soon and the waitress eyeing us with what looked to me to be both envy and disdain and I understood the disdain but not the envy, in fact I wished I was her, leaving at the end of the evening for some place that was mine where the people knew me, welcomed and held me in the sweet embrace of home—oh, nostalgia.

The man was right, the hotel was only a couple of blocks away, and it was cheap, but it was not clean and from the looks of a lot of the people who were standing around in the lobby smoking cigarettes and drinking beer from amber-colored bottles, it was not altogether reputable. Our room overlooked the street and after we took baths in the big tub down the hall, we lay in the one double bed and listened to the Spanish music coming from I didn't know where—a radio, a jukebox. I think I was nearly asleep when I heard June say something about the song that had just begun, she'd heard it before, spics had good music, that was one thing, the chicken wasn't bad either, and that Alberto, he was so fair-skinned. Alberto, I thought to myself, what a nice name.

That night I dreamed a chicken named Alberto was singing about Spic & Span, a funny song that made me laugh myself awake, woke June too, "What the hell's so funny?" she said, part grumpy but part amused. I sang her what I could re-member of the song and the grumpy part got lost as her amusement grew and later she put her head close to mine and hummed the melody softly so when I spoke I spoke softly too. "What's going to happen to us now?" I whis-pered. I whispered it because I wanted an answer so I meant for her to hear, but I didn't want the answer I knew she'd give me, more Ransom Hood nonsense, so maybe it was just as well if she couldn't hear after all. Whether she heard or not, she didn't speak again, she just kept humming that tune in my ear until I fell asleep.

In the morning, there was no singing. June spent seventy-nine cents of the money we had left on emery boards and nail polish and then we had to sit in the car for an extra twenty minutes while her nails dried, twenty minutes during which she never stopped talking, Ransom Ryan this, old Mr. Hood that, and all the while I was praying to myself, please God, please make the man be there and glad to see us and all the rest, which I couldn't even go into because I wasn't sure what all the rest looked like, it seems like my imagination had died with most of my faith, since, to my mind, prayer is sel-dom an act of believing, mostly one of desperation.

But the man wasn't there, in fact they'd never heard of him. This business was run by a Mr. William Turner, actually it was his wife's family's firm, she was a Hood, they were Coral Gables people, but Mr. Turner was from Tampa, and they didn't know anybody named Ransom, what kind of name was that? June fussed with her hair. "It's a very old

Virginia name," she said and then she went on and on about old Virginia and old families, like she believed every word she was saying, but I guess the people in the Hood's office could tell from the way her voice finally trailed off that she didn't, and everybody looked a little embarrassed. June asked if there was a rest room we could use, but I didn't have to go so I sat in a chair and looked unseeing at a magazine until she came back. Before I could even get to my feet she asked if they were giving away any free samples and they said sure and somebody went through a door and came out a couple of minutes later with a bag of marshmallows of every description, including the cookies with pink marshmallows covered in coconut sandwiched between two vanilla wafers.

We got back to the car and June sat herself down and tore right into that bag, opening every single package and taking a bite of first one thing and then another. "What are you doing?" I asked her.

"What does it look like I'm doing?" she said. "I'm having breakfast. Did you ever see so many delicious breakfast treats in your whole life? Which one do you want first?"

It didn't make that big a mess when I knocked the bag out of her hand and then started batting at all the packages that fell onto the car seat and floor because except for the vanilla wafers, these were not foods that made crumbs. I did notice that some of the marshmallow was getting smeared into the ribs of the floormat, but I didn't care. I also didn't care that I knew the sounds I was making were not comprehensible the way words are, they weren't the kind of thing a person could respond to, June couldn't very well say, "Yes, but," or "You don't know what you're talking about," because I was past all that. I was lost to the conviction that we can make ourselves understood and out of understanding will come change, something better.

I think I must have shocked June because for a while she

didn't move a muscle, her mouth stayed slightly ajar, and the last bite of her breakfast was visible on the back of her tongue. But then something took hold of her and she started swatting at every spongy white or pink blob she could get her hands on, streaking it across the windows and the upholstery and the dash, gumming up the dials and the buttons of the radio and the heater.

I guess I saw the door to Hood's office open before June did, but it didn't take her long. Soon a half-dozen people were watching us, one of them laughing, one of them holding herself and not laughing or even looking like she wanted to, the others talking and nodding and shaking their heads, six strangers now witness to our frenzy, that was all it took. June turned the key in the ignition and I put the radio on and folded my hands in my lap and she pulled away from the curb like where we were going was of immense importance and where we'd been meant nothing at all, which in some awful way was the truth.

# Chapter 11

Maybe there's something in gasoline that does it, gets inside people's brains and nerves, it even gets inside their emotions, and calms them down. As the car engine burns the gas, it makes an invisible mist that comes up where the people are riding and after a while everybody gets relaxed. Maybe in some cases, hard ones where the people are really riled up, it takes longer.

It took me and June all that day and into the next before we stopped jumping at every trucker's horn and fighting about radio stations and gas stations and left turns and right turns and wrong turns. And when it got to where we weren't jumping or fighting we grew quiet, except I could hear other people talking, their voices coming from behind my eyes— Lucas and Charlene and Nate and Caroline—and I wanted fervently to be with them and far away from my mother.

It took us a couple of days too, to clean up all the marshmallows from the car, my hands and hair sticky from bits of it in places where you couldn't see it and didn't expect it, and every time one turned up whole, June said the thing that pissed her off was what a waste it had been and if we were hungry we had nobody but ourselves to blame.

By this time she was chain-smoking and living on coffee and tea and Dr Pepper. I got a yen for pineapple juice, though it was too sweet by a year, but then I couldn't get enough of it and I got such a bad case of acid stomach I thought I was gravely ill. I was sitting on the toilet in a fill-ing-station rest room, crying from the pain, doubled over from the cramps, queasy from the smell of too much air freshener and my own rank odor; and June was sitting on the floor beside the stall door singing Theresa Brewer and Patti Page songs.

"Something's wrong with me, I can feel it," I stuttered.

"You just drank too much Del Monte," she said.

"It's not the juice," I said when I finished on the toilet. "Something's wrong with *me*."

June laughed the way you do when what you're thinking isn't funny. "Something's wrong with everything," she said.

Was that so? I asked her and she hesitated for a minute, like she was trying to decide which way she wanted to go with the truth, toward it or away from it, and then she said, "No, no, nothing's wrong. We're fine, you'll see." She put her arm round me and I let myself fall all the way into her to where the truth didn't matter.

June pawned her wedding ring—it turned out that it was worth more than she thought and she said at least Nate hadn't been a cheapskate—and that night we stayed in a run-down cabin beside a lake—I can't remember if it was in Mis-souri or Arkansas. I never once turned in the bed, I slept right through the night and the next morning, and when I woke up in June's arms with her breath soft on the back of my neck, I felt better, I even had an appetite. June said a dish of vanilla pudding was about all I ought to eat. Vanilla pudding sounded good to me. I ate my fill at a diner and then we went back to our cabin and I slept some more and when I woke up it was after dark and we went for a swim.

The water was cold so I waded in slow and I could feel fish slipping between my legs. June floated on her back for the longest time, her hair spread out around her head like seaweed. When she spoke, it sounded as if her voice was coming from the water, it sounded as if the whole lake was talking. "I wish things were different," she said. "I wish I was different."

"How would you be?" I asked, and my voice seemed big too.

She never did answer me. She waved her hands so ripples spread around her. The water lapped at the muddy beach. I floated on my back too, and I wondered how would she be and how would I want her to be? But I couldn't see her different, or me either. It seemed like each of us, June in her way and me in mine, was on some kind of path, our fates coming to meet us like promises we were bound to keep.

We were five or six days out of Tampa, passing through some forgotten town, I think this time we were in northern Arkansas and headed for some place my mother had thought up, when we got pulled over by a policeman for running a red light. It took the two of us to talk him out of giving us a ticket, June going on about a headache, she even managed to squeeze out a few tears, me telling him a story about somebody after us, a crazy Cuban from Tampa who had a patch over one eye and a white boxer dog named Moses.

The young officer patted his tie where it was knotted tight at his throat and ran his thumb over his belt buckle and then he said for us to travel safe. After he drove off we made a bunch of nervous jokes about how good-looking he was. June said I'd done an impressive job of making something up on the spot and since we'd just saved ourselves no less than ten dollars, we ought to spend some of that on dinner.

Two dollars and twenty-five cents bought us a decent meal, roast turkey and mashed potatoes, a slice of coconut custard pie and a couple of cups of hot tea. When we were through, we went for a walk across the street among the markers of a churchyard cemetery. That's where I had it come to me— and I told it all to June—that maybe the people me and her had left were like a trail of dead behind us, and maybe it would always be that way, all the other people in our lives like phantoms that appeared for a while and then faded away, leaving us alone time after time.

June chuckled and shook her head. "You got a unique way of thinking," she said. "I like it."

"But do you think it's so?" I asked her.

She ran her hand over the wings of an angel that marked the grave of William Ward Josephson III. "I don't think it matters whether it's so or not," she said. "I think it's just a special way to put it. I never knew anybody to put things quite the way you do. It's nice."

As we began the walk back to the car, the half moon slipped behind a strip of clouds like a letter slipping into an envelope, and the graveyard grew dark and June tripped and fell on the corner of a small marker sunk deep into the earth.

"You want a hand?" I asked.

"Goddamned grass stains," she said. "I'm okay." She raised herself up off the ground, shook her foot, and started walking again and I followed her.

"Remember that time I stubbed my toe on the crack in the sidewalk downtown?"

"Downtown where?"

"Covington."

"No, I don't remember that."

"June?"

"What?" She turned to look at me and then she looked away. "What?" she asked again when I didn't answer.

"I forget."

I chewed my lip until I could taste blood and then I sucked at it till it stung. I was drinking my blood, it was salty, like the Atlantic Ocean in Vero Beach, and I remembered that first time June took me there and the other places she'd taken me and the places she'd left me and I wondered which was better and which was worse, and finally I thought it wasn't so much a matter of better and worse as it was a matter of what each signified, the varieties of uncertainty. But this was an idea that my still-young mind could not long contain, so I was glad when the moon slipped from behind the clouds and shone down bright again and June smiled.

"Pretty, isn't it?" she said and then she turned to me. "Gosh, you look tired, Lily," she said, and she touched my chin with her hand and I pressed my cheek against her palm to make the touch last.

For a good long while now, we two lived in nearly every circumstance a woman traveling with a girl can manage, and a few we almost couldn't—we spent a night locked up in somebody's garage, we got run off the road by a bunch of Georgia roughnecks and only one of them having an epileptic fit saved us from whatever they had planned. I lost a year of school and June lost a lot of weight and her nails grew discolored and brittle because of the way we ate and the way she smoked. She picked up odd jobs whenever our money started to run low, she sold baby furniture and fresh fish and men's shoes. Sometimes I did too, which was my idea; I worked as a carhop, I washed dishes, I sold souvenirs and cold sodas and tourist maps. The best thing about working was that you got to meet a lot of people, which I was truly thankful for, their stories, the questions they asked, their concern, their presents—a fire-hydrant key chain, a potholder-making kit, and when June laughed at me because I got paid so little money and I had no keys and no pots I ignored her.

We stayed mostly on the outskirts of small towns for a few days, sometimes for a week, then June would get restless, or she'd hear about something she had to see—Natural Bridge, Alabama, the colonial plantations down around Natchez and north along the river. We traveled as far west as Tulsa and as far north as Cincinnati, we saw mountains and rivers and deltas and prairies in every season, we put 25,000 miles on the Buick, despite the bald tires, the flat tires, the radiator overheating, a busted starter, and a mechanic who said he'd give us a complete overhaul if the two of us would go to bed with him. "At the same time?" June asked him as though she was thinking it over seriously.

"I hadn't thought of that," the man yucked, his Adam's apple a red rubber ball popping up and down in his throat.

June looked at me, then she looked away like the shame I was wishing on her had hit its mark. "I wouldn't go to bed with you for a goddamned new car," she snarled at him for my benefit as much as his or her own.

The close calls went down easy compared to a time like this, when June, I knew, would have had us side by side and flat on our backs if I hadn't shown my feelings so plain. These were days when I aimed to live clear of the worst of my thoughts, because how can you face such things? so I tried not to, and most of the time I succeeded. I read the local papers out loud as June drove and I imagined a life for myself in those sleepy little towns. We listened to local radio shows and if they said there was a ball game where we were staying that night, we went, but I always rooted for the home team and she always rooted for the visitors, so it often happened that we weren't hardly talking to each other by the time the game was over. But we usually made up in the coffee shops where everybody went for Cokes after the game because June was quick to switch her allegiances in such company, the football players still wearing their cleats and swollen with their losses same as their wins, June suddenly the greatest authority on passing games and running games and field-goals, and I admit I was in awe of her, how we never paid for a thing those nights, invitations for other nights coming at us from all sides.

"Why not?" I'd ask her later back in our room. "Why can't we stay a while?"

"Stay in this nothing of a place? Not on your life. I got my sights aimed on something big, something fine, and when we get there, you're going to thank me for it, you'll see."

In the morning, she'd take a long time picking out her clothes for the day as though what she wore would determine the shape of our future. Sometimes we'd stop at a Salvation Army store and try on silly clothes, ballgowns, tuxedos, ratty old fur coats, like we were rehearsing for something—the life she imagined for us—though we never bought a thing, in fact we were thinning out our wardrobes. We even drove off and left one suitcase full of clothes at a motel outside of Biloxi and after that, it seemed we didn't need to lug so much around, it got to where the backseat was nearly empty except for a couple of bags filled with June's shoes and the one piece of fabric she still had from the shop in Welch, white cut velvet that had turned yellow around the edges, and when we left Mobile late that summer, June said to toss it in the garbage. "Fancy free," she whooped as we drove away, "footloose and fancy free!"

But I didn't think she felt free. You could hear it in her laughter now, pitched so high and running on like she couldn't stop, she seemed nervous and strained, the same as I

was. How it showed on me was I had nightmares and stomach cramps, and I started to steal things, a ballpoint pen,
some hand cream.

I stole a pair of reading glasses from a drugstore in Marion,
Kentucky, and a box of nonpareils from a candy shop in Lou-
isville. I stole a cheap ankle bracelet from the gift shop at a
truck stop near Demopolis, Alabama, and June about skinned
me alive, chased me into the bathroom and grabbed me by
my hair and told me she was willing to take a lot of chances,
but going to jail wasn't one of them, had I ever thought of
that? and I guess it hit me how vulnerable we were, and it
wasn't just for the thieving. That's when we heard somebody
flush the toilet behind one of the stalls, and the stall door
opened and it was a colored woman. She looked at us and we
looked at her and then June opened the bathroom door to
see who was where they didn't belong, and the sign on the
door said COLORED.

" 'Scuse us," June said to the woman.

"I got the same problem with my girl," the woman said as
we turned to walk out. "Thinks life owes her nice things. I
guess I ought to do like you, raise a fuss, but there's something about it tickles me."

June turned back toward the woman like she was going to
speak, but she just stood there and they looked at each other.
Finally she said, "What's your girl's name?"

"Lucille," the woman answered.

"This is Lily," June said, "and thank you for your words."

A white lady stared at us as we walked out of the rest room
and into the parking lot. "What the hell are you looking at?"
June hollered. When we got in the car, she looked at herself
in the rearview mirror. "Son of a bitch," she said, "I'm just
like that lady."

"About colored?" I asked.

"Uh-huh. And spics and whatever."

After that I didn't steal for a time, and in some strange way it made me feel more optimistic, like if we did what was right, then what was right would come to us. But then a couple of weeks, or maybe it was a month or so later, the funniest thing happened. Me and June were both letting our hair grow, mostly to save the embarrassment of her haircutting. She'd wrecked her bangs so bad she'd made a joke of her own face again and again, and from the last trim she gave me about the time we got to Beulah's house, my hair was so lopsided I swore I could feel my head leaning to one side and my gait favoring the right.

By now June's hair was halfway down her back and a color she called ash-can brown—it turned dark after we left Vero Beach like some people's turns white from fright. Mine grew more side to side than in length and it was blacker than ever. We would sometimes sit for hours in motel rooms and diners, waiting for our hair in curlers to dry, reading Hollywood magazines and trashy newspapers and shocking one another with the stories we read, as though anything could really shock us. Then we'd brush out the sets and try all kinds of styles, twists and buns and beehives.

"My hair is so flyaway," June complained one day. We were standing in the bathroom of the guest cottage we'd taken just outside of Huntsville, it was either Alabama or Tennessee, and we were getting dressed to have supper with a man she'd met in town at the dentist's office where she'd gone to get a tooth pulled. "No matter how many bobby pins I use, some of it always gets loose."

"You need some spray," I said.

"I do," June said. She put on her jacket and jangled the car keys. "I'll be right back."

She came back with hair spray, pulled it out of her pocket, no bag in sight, in fact she'd left her purse and wallet on the bureau. She took off her jacket and repaired her hair style, added a couple of pins, and then she popped the top off the spray and laid down a coat of the stuff so thick I was sure her hair would break if you touched it. "It's Helene Curtis, extra firm," she said when she was finished.

"How much did it cost?"

"It's got a price of sixty-seven cents on it, but I didn't pay a thing."

"You stole it."

"I did. I had to have it and we can't afford it so I took it."

"Well, all right, Lucille," I said, and we laughed.

"You got me there," she said, her lips wet and her eyes shining so I had to shake myself to keep from giving her a peck on the cheek.

Of course later I was glad for my restraint. The man from the dentist's office came to pick us up. His name was Mr. Osgood and he called June Mrs. Wolsey and he called me Miss Wolsey and he was as revolting a person as I'd ever met, talking about the Bible and groping me and June both under the table at the restaurant, crumbs from his dinner roll clinging like bird shit to the stubble of his day-old beard and the front of his dirty white shirt, tomato sauce stuck like dried blood to the corners of his mouth.

But Mrs. June Wolsey didn't bat an eye when he invited us to his house. He said he had something he wanted to show us, it was in the hall where you came in the front door: a little glass case filled with oddities from exotic lands, things like a monkey's paw, a midget's shoe, a pair of shrunken heads, a piece of lava. June made a big fuss over the shrunken heads. She had Mr. Osgood take them out so she could hold them and then she baited him with them, tickling him between the red-skinned folds of his triple chins with the sprouts of black hair.

When he asked us if we wanted to see the other oddities he had upstairs, I said no and June said yes. She set the little heads back in the case, and Mr. O. put on the television in the living room and brought me some milk and a plate of cookies like I was a little girl, which made June double over with laughter. She helped herself to a cookie and said for me to behave myself, young lady, and then she followed him out of the room and up the stairs.

I didn't like any of the shows on TV, except one movie on a channel that was all snow. The sound was okay though, so I listened and tried to follow the story as best as I could, something about a town being invaded by killer bees, and when the floorboards overhead started creaking and groaning, I turned the volume up, I helped myself to some nougat from the kitchen, I wandered around the living room and the dining room and back out to the hall, and I opened the case and looked at the heads some more, they felt like toys in my hand, they were that small.

Small enough, I guess, so they didn't show in my pocket, which is where I put them when I heard June and the man in the hall upstairs, her making some big noise about how much more interesting the upstairs items were than the ones downstairs, the two of them snickering like *they* were children. But when we rode across town in his car, the radio playing opera and a raw wind whipping dead leaves and twigs and whole branches against the parked cars and the windshield of Mr. Osgood's old Chrysler, nobody said a word. And when we got back to the tourist court, June pushed me out fast and she didn't even tell him good night.

It was cold inside our cottage. My mother ran herself a hot bath and I fidgeted with the switch on the electric heater. Something came up, you could smell it, but it wasn't enough to take the chill off the room. My stomach was bound like a fist and the cold was not helping. Finally I gave up on the heat, buried the shrunken heads in a suitcase, and, fully dressed, got under the covers of one of a pair of twin beds, for which I was unspeakably grateful—I was so grateful not to have to lie beside June—and I tried to fall asleep before she finished her bath so I didn't have to talk to her, or listen to her, didn't have to tell her how her doing it—whatever she'd done—with that Mr. Osgood was the lowest, foulest thing ever.

I was still awake when she came out of the bathroom, her hair wrapped in a towel and a cigarette between her lips. "Where'd you put the heads?" she asked me.

"In the suitcase."

"Which one?"

"The tan one."

"Christ sake, Lily," she said as she stubbed out her cigarette in the ashtray on the nightstand. "You are something else."

"You're something else too," I said.

"How come?" she asked.

"Going with him," I said.

"I know," she said. "I know. Good God almighty, I know." She threw her towel across the room and it landed with a wet thud on the top of the bureau. I heard her light another cigarette and blow out the match, heard her taking one drag after another. Then she stubbed out that cigarette too and made a big fuss with her covers and the pillow, flip-flopping this way and that, and she was still going at it when she said, "Christ sake, girl, it's too goddamned late in the day for righteousness, far too late for me, and as long as you're with me it's too late for you too." Then she threw something else across the room, this time aiming for my bed, and making her mark. It was long as my thumb and shaped like a roll of paper. It was a roll of paper money, dollar bills bound with a rubber band, that's what it was, I could see that much when I held it up close to my eyes, though I didn't know how much there was, the room dark and me one hundred percent uninclined to turn on the lamp.

Suddenly, the state of my pillows and covers was as troublesome as June's. I clutched the money tight in my hand and I tossed and I turned but I could not make a place for myself in that damned bed, not then and not later. June didn't sleep much either. I heard her get up to go to the bathroom, smelled her cigarette coming from her side of the room, but I didn't answer when she asked me every couple of hours was I awake.

In the morning when we got up I handed her the money and I said I thought stealing was a better idea and she said I was probably right. "I'm so scared," I said, "and lonely, I'm so lonely and scared."

She nodded her head and she said she didn't wonder. Then she took the rubber band from around the roll of money and she counted it. It was $25, fifteen curly singles and two curly five-dollar bills. She made a face of disgust and a sound to go with it and then she said, "Me too."

# Chapter 12

I think it was at about this time that June taught me to drive, and I have to say I took to it like I had high-test running in my veins. I was a real fancy dancer, the way I moved from lane to lane, I even learned how to pop the clutch and parallel park. And now me and her had something else to bicker about, who was going to drive, but since she was the only one with a license, she usually won. On the other hand, no matter who was driving we had equal say about which roads to take, this a small victory for me, even though no matter who was pointing the way, we'd still sometimes end up on a road we'd been on before, and some roads we were on again and again so it felt like we were following ourselves, like spies. We also disagreed about people whose names we were unsure of, about trees—was it a hickory or a chinaberry?—about windshield-wiper blades and gas caps and tire pressure. Of course most of what we were fighting about wasn't really what was wrong between us, but I must have known somewhere deep inside myself that the real wrongs couldn't be righted, and if they couldn't be righted then they couldn't be faced, better to look at something else instead.

As it turned out, I had to admit that except for Mr. Osgood, boys and men were usually a good distraction. I'd already learned that I could be sassy as June when I wanted to be. And it gave me a kick, I guess in part because it gave her a kick to see it, so every now and then I'd lay it on thick, coming on to anyone I thought was even halfway good-looking, and the truth was, he didn't really have to be good-looking, he just had to have some little thing, like the way he smiled or the way he walked, so that after we'd enjoyed his hospitality for a meal or a night or a weekend on the town, and no matter how boring or rude or frightening he'd turned out to be, one of us could still say, "Well, he did have the sweetest way about him," and the other one could say, "He did, didn't he?" Then we'd both laugh, and sometimes, when there was what June called booty, we'd remind each other how his bad jokes, his bad breath, his horrid manners, a couple of near misses with men who were scary or just plain weird, had all been worth it—there was the free food and the gifts and sometimes the little things one of us snuck into a pocket from his bathroom or his kitchen or the living room, a dresser scarf, a handful of change, some pearl earrings, a silver picture frame, a pair of crystal salt-and-pepper-shakers. It was like we were getting something for nothing, was the way June liked to look at it, and I went along with her because it was exactly like she said, I'd already gone so far and I couldn't see any place else to go.

I turned fourteen that spring. We were in Greenwood, Mississippi, on my birthday, and everything looked lush and green; besides the lilacs and the azaleas, there was rhododendron in full bloom, white and pink and purple, all that color like the hand that turns the knife that lives in your heart year round so you mostly don't feel it but the sudden twist of springtime makes sure you do.

We were sitting at the counter of a coffee shop eating french fries and gravy and reading the comic strips from an old Sunday paper. June asked the waitress for more hot water for her tea, and then she asked me if I was done with that page. I said no, I was only halfway through Beetle Bailey, and she sighed real loud like waiting another couple of minutes to read Blondie would do her in. Then she started to talk about our finances, how we were down to forty dollars, she thought she had to have another tooth pulled, and the Buick needed new brakes. I finished Beetle Bailey and turned the page of the paper and she said, "I'm going to sell the car."

"You're not either," I said.

"I am too," she said. "Besides the brakes being shot, the clutch is about to go, so is second gear. If we keep the damned thing, I've got to renew the registration and pay an insurance premium and get it inspected, and I don't want to do all that, spend all that money, when I could be making it. I'm going to sell the damned car and we're going to ride around in buses and trains like a couple of hot shots. Club cars, sleeper cars, porters, the whole bit."

Wasn't it because I was just learning to drive? Wasn't it that she couldn't stand for me to show off with my smooth shifts and my sure left-hand turns? But even if I never drove that car again, it was where I lived. I knew every scratch on the dashboard and the windows, every tuck and button of the upholstery. I knew how to set the windows, driver's and passenger's side alike, at just the right angle to get just the right amount of air on my face, and how best to set myself against the door for sleeping. And when the car's day on the road ended and the hum of its motor was stopped, I could hear it for hours afterward, like it was still talking to me.

"We could sell some of our stuff," I said as I turned the page again.

"What stuff?"

"The salt-and-pepper-shakers, those earrings, the shrunken heads."

"Huh," she snorted, "the heads were worthless and I already sold the rest."

I closed the paper and called to the waitress for another cup of tea. She asked me did I want more hot water and I said, "Give me a fresh tea bag. And some heavy cream, if you've got it." I stirred too much cream and a couple of spoonfuls of sugar into the hot tea and then I slurped it from the lip of the cup, still sitting in the saucer on the counter. "It's not yours," I said to June. "The car's not yours."

"What the hell are you talking about?" she snarled.

"It's *our* car, you can't just sell it. Hell, it's *Nate's* car. You don't want it anymore, you got to give it back to him."

"You fucking little jerk," she said in a voice filled with so much hate I was sure she'd hit me. Then I remembered times when I'd feared Caroline might hit me too and how she never had, never, and neither had Nate, and there I was in some cheesy little coffee shop eating french fries and gravy and drinking my tea too hot and too light, thinking about my father and my grandmother, neither of whom I'd seen or spoken to in nearly two years and it was my goddamned birthday, for Christ sake, and June hadn't even said anything or bought me a present, nothing, and never mind my birthday a year ago, please God, never mind it, because was it already a whole year. It seemed like it was only a day ago or else it had never happened, the year had *not* come and gone, or it had and maybe that was why I was feeling the lunch counter tilt and me with it.

She didn't hit me. She lit a cigarette and she smoked it

hard and laid into me like words were weapons. What a dumb-assed fool I was. Did I think it was my goddamned father's car? Fine, then I could sit myself down behind the son-of-a-bitch wheel and drive myself right on back to him, but by the way, just where in hell was I going to go? Where did I think I'd find him? Of course I could go back and wait for him in Covington, since it was clear from that phone call back at Beulah's house that Caroline was just dying to see me. And wasn't that what had happened all those times I'd called her when we were staying with Sally and Neil? Christ sake, did I think nobody noticed all those calls to Covington, and she'd paid for them, every single one of them, one lousy minute apiece, because I hadn't bothered to reverse the charges back then, and you know we sure could have used that money, maybe if the telephone bills hadn't cost so much, we wouldn't have to sell the Buick now—on and on she went, her voice far too loud, the waitress just looking at us at first, but finally she asked June if she could either talk a little quieter or talk somewhere else.

That was the perfect excuse for my mother to dump what was left of our breakfast onto the counter and leave without paying the bill. I followed her out, but not across the street to where the car was parked, so when she got in and turned the key in the ignition and rolled down the window and hollered to me that I'd better move my ass if I was coming with her, I was already halfway down the block walking in the opposite direction, and when I turned to look, the Buick was out of sight.

I spent my fourteenth birthday in a park at the far end of town. At first I sat in a daze, sick to my stomach, tormented by clothes that suddenly felt three sizes too small. The thing that most distressed me was that it seemed like June thought when I'd made those calls to Caroline from Welch it had been my grandmother who'd hung up on me like she had when I called her from Vero Beach. But it was *me* that hung up all the times before, so it was no wonder Caroline had done it back to me that spring. Now I saw how I'd brought on our suffering. This was an idea that vexed me deeply, because with it came the vague notion that I might do things another way, although I had no idea what that way might be. So I cursed the birds and the stray dogs and cats, and then I fell asleep in the shade beside a fountain.

When I woke up I felt clearer-headed and my stomach had quieted down. The park was starting to get crowded now. I talked to some people I met, mothers with their babies, later on there were kids on their way home from school, men out of work, older ladies in pairs who shared benches with me and asked me about myself, where had I been, was I traveling alone? I told them that I was from Albuquerque, and that I'd been traveling by myself for ten years. Everybody knew I was lying, but nobody bothered me about it and in a funny way I even began to enjoy my make-believe life and the feeling it gave me, I was breathing deeper and I felt easier in my clothes.

People offered me things to eat from their paper bags and purses, halves of sandwich halves and fruit and nuts and candy, and some of them told me their stories too, about neighbors and families and vacations they had taken to Japan and the Grand Canyon. One man told me about a trip he took to Nashville to visit the Grand Ole Opry. He said he'd walked all the way and it was the high point of his life. He believed everybody had a journey they had to take in order to find out who they were. "But you know about that, don't you?" he said to me, which pissed me off no end, because I didn't like to consider that I didn't know who I was, which wasn't what he meant but it was all I could hear. The man folded his newspaper and wiped his fingers on his handkerchief and headed back out of the park in the direction he'd come from, leaving me to fuss with his words: Was that what me and June had been doing, finding out who we were, because who was anybody? Who the hell was anybody?

Late in the afternoon, an elderly couple invited me to their house for supper. The lady said she'd never seen me in town before and she asked me where was I from. Albuquerque didn't seem like the right answer that time. I wanted to tell her the truth, but I wasn't sure how far back to go and I said so. Why didn't I just start at the beginning? her husband asked me, so I did, I began with Covington and then Welch and all the places we'd stopped on our way south and then Vero Beach and Tampa, which is where I was when the old lady said she didn't mean to interrupt me, but just hearing about all that traveling wore her out, she herself liked to go home at night, did I want to be their guest? She didn't like to leave me there by myself, they had an extra room they could make up for me if I wanted to stay the night, and I said no, but thank you just the same.

The old couple left and I sat and listened to some stupid damned song I hated coming from the other side of the trees where somebody was sitting in a parked car and playing the radio. I tried thinking hard so I wouldn't hear the music, but that only made me feel worse because all my thoughts were questions I'd feared for so long—what if June had left me for good and I was truly alone? What would happen to me? How could I make my way?—questions I'd asked myself before, but I was only half listening then. Now they sounded so loud in my head I feared somebody else might hear them too and I looked around to see if anybody was listening.

I waited until after dark and then I followed the old couple's directions to the bus station and there was June, sitting in a chair, smoking a cigarette, reading a magazine and eating Good & Plenty, our two biggest suitcases, an overnight case and a big shopping bag beside her on the floor. She tried to look like she didn't see me coming in the door, and I tried to pretend that I didn't notice her either, until I was already sitting right near her, only one chair between us where she had a sweater and her purse. She put out her cigarette in the sand-filled ashtray next to her chair and started talking, her eyes still fixed on the magazine.

"I got a good price for the car, and the dentist said the tooth was worth saving so he gave me a cheap filling." She pointed to the suitcases beside her. "I had to take a lot of our things to the Goodwill. I had to give away some of your clothes, I hope I did all right." She put the magazine down and took out a big gift box from the shopping bag. It was wrapped in pink paper with frilly pink ribbon all over the top. "I got you this present," she said. "I got you a little birthday cake too, an ice-cream cake, but it melted and I had to throw it away."

My hands were cold but my face was hot for all the things I had and hadn't said and done that day and now for all the things my mother was saying and not saying too. A lame colored man whistled "The Battle Hymn of the Republic" and pushed a cleaning cart across the far side of the room, dragging a mop and a broom behind him. I kept my eyes on him when I spoke. "What flavor did you get me?"

"Chocolate," she said and she smiled, I could hear the smile in her voice though I was still looking at the old man.

"Chocolate?"

"Uh-huh. With chocolate sprinkles and your name written on it."

"My name?"

" 'Happy Birthday, Lily,' that's what it said."

"Did you eat some of it?"

"I had a little."

"Was it good?"

"It was delicious." I turned toward her now and watched

her light the wrong end of a cigarette. The smell of the burning filter tore at the back of my throat. She lit the right end of a second one and tapped the tip on the rim of the ashtray. "Aren't you going to open your present?"

A girl a couple of years older than me got up from a seat across the way and came to watch as I set the gift in my lap and pulled off the bows, tore the wrapping, lifted off the top of the box, and opened the white tissue paper. "What is it?" I asked, holding up a white shirtwaist dress.

"It's a dress," the girl said. "Prettiest dress in town. I saw it in the shop window at High Society."

"I'm sure it's your size," June said. "I tried it on and it was a little short for me and a little tight at the waist, so I think it will fit you."

I went into the ladies' room and I put the dress on, though it took me a while to get it zipped up and buttoned with my hands all thumbs and my heart slamming against my chest like a ball at a paddle. The length was right and the waist was right too, and I guess I surprised myself some when I saw in the mirror how shapely I looked in it, even though the skirt was full and the top where the darts were was a little big on me. But it wasn't so much the fit of the dress that surprised me, it was seeing my own face above it, not June's, like hers was still the one I expected. But no, there was my frizzy black hair and my green eyes open wide, and this time, though it was for just an instant, the sight of my own reflection stopped me cold, as though in recognizing myself, I'd seen through to something deeper inside me, and the sight of it shook me to my roots.

"Just look at you," June said from the door to the rest room. "Don't you look fine? The white's nice on you, brings out the color of your eyes. You ought to wear more white, wear mine, you can try some things on when we get to . . ." She didn't finish her sentence. She crossed her arms over her chest and I did the same. "Horrible lighting in these rest rooms," she said. Then she walked up close to the mirror and examined herself while she spoke. "I'll tell you the truth, I was worried sick. I didn't know where to look for you, I didn't want to go to the police because the whole thing was so goddamned foolish . . ." Her top lip swelled up and tears streamed down her face. She turned and put her arms around me and I could feel her small breasts against mine and her ribs surprisingly fine and delicate. "Don't let me go," she whispered, "you're all I got." I held her real loose so she wouldn't feel me shaking. After a while she said, "I left that girl with our things. We better go back outside."

Shaking still, even though the glimpse I'd had of myself was already fading, I took off the dress and put it in the box and put my other clothes back on and then I went first and June followed me back out to where the girl was sitting with our bags. I looked at the clock, it was half-past nine. On the board that listed bus arrivals and departures, I read that the next bus leaving town was not for another seven hours.

"Guess I'll go on home," the girl said, brushing each of our suitcases with the back of her knuckles like she was telling them good bye too. Then she wished me a happy birthday and walked out the door. I watched her disappear beyond the couple of buses parked in the lot.

It was quiet in the station now the cleaning man had gone too. June filed her nails and I tried to read her magazine, though my mind wandered the way it does when you are trying to figure something out in your head, your fate. I think we both slept some. Around midnight I got hungry and she dug a couple of foil-wrapped bologna sandwiches out of the shopping bag.

We left on the 4:40 A.M. bus to Atlanta with a pair of special one-way tickets that let us make as many stops along the way as we liked. I turned to the bus window, a black mirror that showed me to myself once again, vaguer, less distinct than what I'd seen in the rest room. June balled up her sweater for a pillow and set it against me, laid her head there, and shut her eyes.

# Chapter 13

You can buy a ticket from Greenwood to Atlanta, but that doesn't mean the bus leaving Greenwood is going to Atlanta. That's what the driver explained to us when our bus went as far as Tuscaloosa and everybody got off. The funny thing is, I'd looked at that bus before we got on it, looked at the place above the windshield where it names the bus's final destination, and it did say Tuscaloosa, but I figured that they'd made a mistake. When you have it in your mind that you know where you're going, even Greyhound can't convince you otherwise.

So we stayed in Tuscaloosa for a couple of days in a hotel near the bus depot. June looked for me to give her an argument about being there, since we hadn't meant to be, and then being in Montgomery and Knoxville and Lexington and Cincinnati, which are just some of the big cities that weren't on the way to Atlanta, and there were lots of small ones too, all of which we drifted in and out of over the next couple of months. But strange to tell, this new kind of drifting was okay with me. The landscape outside the windows of the buses we rode was a beautiful blur of color and light. I felt like I was moving in slow motion, one day spilling seamlessly into the next, time a long-forgotten wound so nothing seemed to bother me, not even my hormones—because I got my first period about then.

Of course I hated the huge pad wadded between my legs and June fussing at me to change it, to wash, and besides all that she wanted to watch. "I can do it myself," I told her.

"I know you can," she said. "I just want to see you're doing it right."

But even if she trailed me across a diner to the rest room, I closed and locked the door to keep her out, so I could have it for myself, because never mind the pad, it was *my* blood, *my* few fine pubic hairs gritty and crusty, *my* sex and smell so new.

But then that summer, everything seemed new, and I thought maybe we were headed for a change, I was feeling downright optimistic, though when I asked myself what it might look like, the change we were headed for, I couldn't say, but maybe that didn't really matter, because now I had this idea: that me and my mother were on a journey. We weren't just wandering aimlessly, we were looking for something, we were finding out who we were, and I liked us more, I liked myself better for it. I liked the dreary hotel rooms better than the road places where we'd stayed when we'd been driving ourselves; I liked the sleepy front-desk clerks and the pompous bus drivers and the quarrelsome ticket agents and the intoxicating diesel fuel and the bad food. I liked riding trains at night, when the hills were gentle shadows against the sky and the lights in people's houses made me wonder about their lives; I liked riding buses in the daytime, when it was raining or the roads were dusty or they were working on a bridge and we had to sit for twenty minutes while a cement mixer poured tons of the stuff down its chute into a big hole in the ground.

Sometimes we'd meet people who offered us rides and if they didn't June asked them and they usually said yes. We rode to Shreveport and back with a lady who drove a 1941 Packard and sold Bibles door to door. Sarah was her name, and she and June hit it off because Sarah wore white all the time too, and they had bleach and blueing to talk about, which helped my mother avoid the obvious subject: Bibles, religion, God. We rode to Montgomery with a pair of newly-weds, Kay and Carter. June didn't want to go with them at first but I begged and pleaded like it meant the world to me, but it was swaying her that gave me such a thrill.

We rode in farm trucks and salesmen's sedans, in a preacher's station wagon. We met some people who were traveling in a caravan of fifteen vehicles of all sorts and we rode with them for a bit and stayed with them in a tent one night and they asked if we wanted to join them, but when we heard they were headed for the Canadian Rockies we said no thank you, it would be midsummer by the time they got there, but June said it would still be too cold for us, especially the nights, which was a real disappointment to me because I liked them a lot, they were kind and gentle people. But then we rode in a little foreign sports car convertible, a Triumph, that belonged to a boy named Theodore Compson, Theo for short, and I liked him, too.

We met him one morning in downtown Vicksburg. He had a sterling silver flask filled with Jack Daniel's and he picked me and June up in front of the public library where we'd gone to settle an argument, something about the Civil War, something about slavery and emancipation. Whatever we'd found in the library hadn't helped though, and we were still going at it when we stopped at the corner for a red light.

Theo was stopped at the same light with his top down and his striped tie flung over his shoulder. "Afternoon, ladies," he said.

"Same to you," I said. "Fine-looking car," I added, stretching fine out to make it say more.

The light turned green. Theo crossed the intersection, pulled up beside the curb, and waited for us to cross the street. "I'm just out for a spin," he said, as we came up alongside of him. "Is there someplace I can drive you ladies?"

June nestled into the seat beside him and I crammed into the little seat in back, leaning up between them, smelling his aftershave, feeling the glow from his smile and his breath raw with bourbon. He took us all over hell and gone that afternoon, through small towns and villages, down beautiful tree-lined streets to look at white-columned houses, past churches and fine stores and all the while I was flirting with him like I knew what I was doing, which of course I did. And he was flirting back too, shooting me smiles and winks in the rearview mirror, squeezing my knee and playing with June about her daughter and June drank from his flask, tugged at her ponytail, touched his arm, talked endlessly about herself, and laughed, but I didn't mind, me and Theo were laughing too.

When we all got hungry he took us to his daddy's country club for lunch. White and green, white and green, white brick and white awnings and green carpeting and green lawn, acres of it, and big old leafy trees. Everybody was wearing white, white shoes and white dresses and pants and jackets, all of them stinking rich, all of them, that is except for the colored help, dressed in starched white uniforms, green aprons stiff and ruffled, jackets with brass buttons and braided green trim. Though June at least was wearing white head to toe, the two of us looked a little ragged beside the other guests, but Theo didn't seem to mind. He had a

crooked smile that I couldn't get enough of. I guess he enjoyed my smile too, teased me about curly hair. June smiled
right along with us, picked at her cuticles.

I never knew there was food as good as what we had,
shrimp cocktail, something called lobster thermidor, strawberry shortcake with whipped cream piled ten inches high,
and it would have been a perfect meal except for this one
thing: a colored man with gray hair at his temples served us
from a brass-trimmed wooden cart and you never heard such
manners, such deference, and it mortified me so, but when I
tried to be nice to him, June took another long swallow of
her whiskey sour and then she said, "Is there something you
need, Lily? You ask Theo," and she gave my hand a touch to
let me know it wasn't proper to fuss with him or the handsome young colored boy who cleared our soup dishes. What
made it even worse was that for some reason I thought for
sure Theo was feeling the same mortification as me, but
when I looked at him, he just nodded his head and smiled,
which made my head swim because I loved his smile, but I
hated what it concealed.

When we were through eating, Theo signed for our lunch
and then he took us on a tour, and though I didn't like to
admit it, the place was grand, there was a ballroom and tennis
courts, and a swimming pool big as a football field. Did June
want to take a dip? he offered, it might be refreshing. She
said she didn't have her suit with her and he said that was no
problem. He showed her to the ladies' changing rooms, got
the attendant to give her a loaner, told her we'd meet her
outside, grabbed my hand, and off we ran.

Oh, I had myself a time. I sat in the seat beside him and we
drove way out into the hills and bought a tin of spoon bread
from a farmer's wife and washed it down with what was left
in his flask and swam in the woman's pond and did it right
there in the grass, and when we were through we listened to

the birds on the far side of the pond and the cows moaning in the meadow beyond the trees. When he got hard again and came up inside me, I could hear the woman calling her chickens by name and one of them was Lily and me and Theo laughed so hard he popped right out of me, but then he put himself back where he'd been, only deeper, surer, sure as me when I opened my mouth and called out my own name.

Later on we swam once more and Theo dried me off with his white shirt and then he put it on wet so it stuck to his chest. I couldn't help but stare at his little berry nipples hard behind the cotton, and I thought about Lucas and how pretty boys and men are and I thought about Nate and I felt confused about him, was it all right to think about him with the others, and what about the others, all the men me and June had gone with? I'd scorned her for it, but here I was with Theo and was there any difference between me and her now?

Theo must have seen me staring absently at his chest because he brought me back to him with a tweak to each of the new swells on mine. "We're just about the same size," he said, "but I like yours better." His teasing touch made me ache for more of him, even as we were waving good-bye to the farmer woman.

Back at the car, Theo asked me did I want to drive. Did I ever—I sprayed sand and grit from the rear tires as I pulled onto the road. We sang farm songs, "The Farmer in the Dell," "Old MacDonald," and "She'll Be Coming 'Round the Mountain." When my hair dried big around my head, Theo grabbed it by the handful. "God, you're gorgeous," he said, and I made him say the word over and over for the sheer pleasure of hearing it. "Was this your first time, Gorgeous?" he said and I said it was, and he said, "How did you like it?" and I said I liked it fine, and I did, it was like a beautiful dream.

It was half past six when we got back to the country club. June was sitting at the bar on the terrace smoking a cigarette, drinking a whiskey sour, talking with the bartender, smiling big. When she saw us she waved and her mouth stretched a little tighter across her face and then she was all gracious talk when we were standing there beside her, what a wonderful afternoon she'd had, the very thing she needed, the most interesting people, so refined, she'd have so much to tell our hosts that evening, oh, hadn't I mentioned to Theo that we were staying in town and having dinner at the home of some friends, they were picking us up around eight, in fact if he didn't mind too much, could he just run us back to our hotel?

She gave the bartender's hand a coy touch and out at the car she took her place in the front seat like it had her name on it, still talking, such geniality, "Thank you, Theo, you have been an absolute godsend this afternoon, otherwise it would have been the dreariest day, don't bother pulling up in front of the hotel, right here is fine, we have to pick something up at the drugstore." She kissed him good-bye, first on the cheek and then on his lips, and she strutted into the pharmacy with a proprietary air.

Theo reached back and wrapped his arms around my neck and pulled me to him. We kissed just once and then he asked when we'd be leaving town and I said probably in the morning. He said that's what he figured, which made me feel the humiliation he must have sensed because he bent my head toward him and kissed first one eyelid and then the other and he said he was smart enough to know that things aren't always the way they looked to be.

I found June inside at the magazine stand reading *True Confessions* and eating a piece of peanut brittle. I came up beside her to look over her shoulder, pretending that I wasn't confused and scared and excited, making believe that my heart wasn't pounding loud in my chest, but she must have heard it because she spun around and dropped the magazine and raised her hand with her palm open to smack me like a smack could silence a heart. I grabbed her wrist so tight I could feel her bones and tendons like gristle under my thumb and the pupils of her eyes grew little like pinholes and neither one of us said a word.

We had a room at a hotel behind the bus station. There was no lobby, just a dingy second-floor office tended by a middle-aged woman with dyed black hair and a tight black crepe dress with the black hanger ribbons trailing out of the armholes. She looked up from a magazine as we walked past her. "Good night," she called and June called back, "Not likely."

It was still light out, not even seven according to the clock I'd seen in a store window around the corner. June sat in the chair beside the window and lit a cigarette and I grabbed a towel and went down the hall to the bathroom. I sank myself in the tub up to my nose, listened to my heart grow quiet, and watched the light fade through the mottled glass of the window, Theo's name and mine lapping at the sides of the tub when I stirred.

It was pitch-dark outside and only a single bare bulb lit the hall as I made my way back to our room. I opened the door and the first and only thing I saw as I stood there, still clutching the doorknob, was June gone, two of our bags gone too, two twenty-dollar bills and a note stuck with lipstick to the mirror above the dresser. "I'm going back to Tampa on the eight o'clock bus. Alberto's number is 555-7076. There's another bus leaving in the morning. It takes a good while to get there, but I bet you can use the time."

I made myself walk slow, down the corridor the other way now, past the pay telephone June must have used to make her travel plans while I was having my bath, and out to the office where the lady with the dyed black hair was sleeping in her chair. She had a radio on, Gogi Grant too loud so I had to shout to make myself heard over "The Wayward Wind." She woke with a start and wiped her mouth like she was checking to see if she'd spewed a trail of drool. "What'd you say?" she asked nervously.

"What time is it," I said, "I just asked did you know what time is it."

She looked down to the small gold watch pinned to her dress, squinted to read its tiny face. "Does eight-thirty sound right to you?"

It did, it sounded exactly right. But then what difference did it make what time it was? Even if the bus hadn't left yet, and even if I could get to the station before it did, what would I say to her? Not *I'm sorry*. Not *take me with you*. I couldn't say any of the things a person might say to fix it between us, because I was scared but I was angry too, and maybe at that moment my anger was bigger than my fear, maybe that's what comes with having a name and a face of your own, and an afternoon for yourself, one lousy afternoon, June, that was all it was, so I couldn't say those nice things, nor could I say *go to hell*, since if that was what I had to say, why hurry over there?

Of course none of this mattered, because it *was* too late, but back in our room the hour didn't keep me from pacing the floor and talking out loud to myself, tearing at the bedclothes, pounding the wall with my fists, with my head, wearing myself out long after a man's voice from the hall told me to shut up, people were trying to sleep, I must be out of my mind.

And the bus ride to Tampa was worse. I hardly ate a thing because the anger had faded, and now I was afraid. I was afraid to spend the change from the ticket at the places where we stopped for something to eat, and I was afraid to sleep, though the ever-wakeful hours were awash with dread that felt the same no matter what I imagined about my future, dread of finding June, dread of not finding her.

I was exhausted and famished when I got off that bus, still uncertain in my mind, praying to God to make her be there, praying to God to take her from me. But then there she was at the station and all uncertainty was gone. I nearly fainted at the sight of her, her arms strong around me, my legs wobbly, my mouth dry, our eyes finding each other again and again and losing each other in an instant the way it happens when you're on the edge of something big and new but your life is grabbing at you, pulling you backward.

She bought me breakfast at a coffee shop across the street from the station and we talked mostly about the weather. Then we took the city bus to a little town outside of Tampa where June had already rented a room from a widow whose children were all grown. I napped on and off for the best part of the day and when I woke up well into the night, I was hungry. June made me a jelly omelette and some toast and we sat in a couple of rocking chairs on the front porch of the white brick house and watched the lights from the city glow in the sky. "There's excitement over there, that's what I come here for," she said. Then she turned to me. "What'd you come for?"

When I spoke, I hardly knew my own voice. It was flat and beat. "I come for you," I said.

"Good," June said. "Good that you know it." She took a deep breath, let it out slowly, tapped her finger on the arm of the rocker. "I didn't like to have to remind you, but there was nothing else to do." She lit a cigarette and got up from her chair and walked to the door. Then she stopped and she turned to me and she said, "All along, I seen it coming, what with one thing or another, but I tried to give you the benefit of a doubt. It was your running off with Theo like you did that made me decide once and for all that you were getting too used to having your own way."

And that was the thing I tried to make sense of after she went to bed and I sat on in the rocker, because what *was* my way? What did it look like, and how would I know it if I saw it? Then I remembered what Beulah Younger had said when she'd read my star chart, how I was going to have to choose between what I was given and what I created, and I knew right then that June's way was what I'd been given and my way was what I made and I was stuck dead in the middle between the two.

# Chapter 14

We stayed on in Tampa for a while, and all things considered, it seemed like we had a decent situation. June got work at Alberto's cigar factory in the part of Tampa we'd been in the year before, Ybor City. Everybody else who worked there was Cuban, mostly they had dark hair and dark skin and some of them were colored people and they spoke Spanish, all of which June said reminded her of Vero Beach and the killing frost and being broke, but this was different because Alberto said she'd be making good money soon. The way he explained it, even though sorting tobacco paid the best, that was a job for the men, but before long he was going to have her learn to roll, then she'd be making a good hourly wage. In the meantime she was working in the office, the book-keeper needed help, it was nice to have a girl around who spoke good English, and this way he could keep an eye on her, which June said could turn out to pay better than sorting or rolling or anything else that had to do with cigars.

During the day I helped the widow with the babies she

took in for working mothers. I had my favorites among them, a cross-eyed little girl named Hyacinth, another girl named Bessie, who ate the dirt in the yard. The widow said I had a nice way with the children and regretted she couldn't afford to pay me a little something. I didn't tell her how glad I was to be useful, to sing to the infants and play patty-cake with the toddlers. They kept me busy and out of the way of my own futile restlessness, better not to think too much about me and June and how it was between us now, polite, courteous—maybe formal is what I mean. And me resigned to the ways that seemed least likely to cause friction between us, this formality like a fulcrum upon which we balanced ourselves, though it clearly favored June, her end of the beam shorter for the far greater weight she carried.

Fortunately, besides the children I found other comforts there. We sometimes went for walks with the widow in the evening and the three of us watched games of shuffleboard and horseshoes. Though the Gulf of Mexico was a few miles away, you could smell it in the air and hear the sound of the wind in the sawgrass and the palmettos. Vero Beach was the last place we'd stayed for more than a week or two, and I remembered it now with affection.

A couple of men who lived in a house a few blocks away came and sat on the porch with us Friday and Saturday nights, drinking cold beers and joking with June, June joking back. I did too, or at least I meant to, but I guess it showed that I didn't have much to give to it and one night after they'd left, June said she'd like it if I tried a little harder to make the men feel welcome. I said I'd try and June said she knew I would, but they never came back again.

A couple of times Alberto invited June to supper at a Spanish place on the bay where they ate pork chops and rice and black beans and that same sweet yellow custard, that flan, the waitress had served us, and afterward they sat outside under a huge poinsettia tree and he smoked what he called a panatella.

"What's a panatella?" I asked. We were doing our wash at a Laundromat a couple of blocks from our room. The place was empty except for another lady whose clothes looked as gray when she took them out of the machine as they'd looked when she put them in.

"It's a kind of cigar," June said. "Classy, that's what Alberto calls it."

"Cigars make an awful smell," I said.

"Shut your mouth," June said with a big grin on her face. "As long as they're paying our rent they smell like roses."

She did bring a smell home in her clothes, it wasn't roses but it *was* kind of sweet. June said it was from the tobacco, and that the streets around all the cigar factories smelled that same way, sweet and rich, like something delicious except it wasn't for eating, though it did make you hungry, June said, it did give you an appetite.

After we'd been there close to a month, I'd every now and then take the bus downtown around four o'clock to meet June and Alberto at the factory and we'd ride in his Lincoln Continental to a nice restaurant and eat Cuban food and I found I was genuinely happy to see him again. His manners were so fine, he was a gentleman, that was for sure, and if I couldn't always understand him, I usually knew what he was saying because his eyes were so expressive. He wore beautiful shoes and a fancy diamond watch and his nails were manicured, and though he didn't look the least like Nate, I liked to believe that Nate looked like him, the shoes, the watch, his nails shiny too.

Alberto didn't like for June to smoke cigarettes, he said it was bad for business, so he gave her cigarillos. She'd wear her white sundress, and the white big-brimmed straw hat and the sunglasses he'd bought her and sip a rum and soda and smoke those long skinny things that looked like twigs between her fingers, and when she was with him, she had a way of laughing with her head thrown back and even I could see how beautiful she looked, and how he talked to her like she was a lady and stood when she got up from the table to go to the rest room, and while she was gone he spoke only of her, and when she came back he stood again and pushed her chair in and I could see sweat pooling under his eyes and making his clean white shirt stick to his chest, the heat between them boiling over.

After we finished our meal, Alberto would take me and June by the arm and the three of us would go for a slow stroll among the crowded narrow streets of Ybor City. There was Spanish movies and Spanish music on the radios and jukeboxes and Spanish newspapers and Spanish people wherever you looked, and despite my intentions, it got to where I thought all of it together, that place and those people and, yes, June and Alberto and heat and sex and love, was like what I'd had with Theo, like a beautiful dream.

Alberto had a friend named Luis Weinberg, who joined us one night. We went to a restaurant where there was music; men in tight black pants played horns and drums and guitars fast and loud, and one man in white pants and a white shirt with puffy, lace-frilled sleeves sang with his fists clenched tight by his sides, and everyone danced like doomsday was coming and there was nothing to save yourself for.

Dark-skinned, Luis was, with black hair and velvety black eyes. I guess he took a real shine to me, that's what June said when we went to the ladies' room, and she told me I didn't have to be shy with the man, never mind that he had a Jewish name and how he was so dark he nearly looked colored, because he owned another cigar factory and he had plenty of money. It wasn't Luis's color or his name that bothered me, of course not, it was how June talked about him that made my stomach turn. I didn't like her prejudice in the first place and wasn't Nate one-quarter Jewish and me one-eighth? But I was used to that. What bothered me most was seeing that money could buy her out of it, and now I guessed I knew what tobacco made her hungry for.

When we got back to our table, Alberto said he wanted to dance. Luis said he needed to stretch his legs and asked me if I'd care to join him on the patio. I looked at June and she laughed that dreadful wonderful laugh. "Go ahead, Sugar," she said. "Girl of eighteen can take care of herself fine."

Just then a woman selling gardenias stopped at our table. Luis asked if I wanted one, and I said no thank you. He tipped the girl anyway and I looked at June and then I looked away. Luis petted my head and I got crazy sad and happy that such a handsome grown man was paying me so much attention. Then the band played a song that made everybody wild and June and Alberto danced as wild as the rest of them and Luis took me by the hand and led me to the terrace. I was glad to be away from the crowd, and the music sounded better at that distance. Luis asked a waiter to bring us two glasses of some kind of Cuban soft drink. Then he lit a small cigar and smiled at me. "I don't think you are eighteen," he said.

I steadied myself as I gripped the railing and I said, "I'm not."

He coiled a curl of my hair around his finger. "You don't mind?" he asked.

"No."

For the next couple of days, June went to work early and stayed out late, and then that Friday evening she and Alberto and Luis came to get me and we went to the Columbia. It was the biggest restaurant I'd ever seen, seven dining rooms and five bars, and one bar where they had a special tradition: when you ordered champagne, they served it to you at your table, poured it into the top one of four glasses stacked each atop the other, so when that one was full, it spilled over into the one underneath it, and when that one filled, the champagne spilled over to the next one, so it made a fountain. June did like Alberto and Luis showed her, leaned across the table and let the fountain spill into her mouth, and we were all laughing when somebody said let Lily try. Luis had his arm around me. Now he took hold of me gently by the back of my neck and he said, "No, she's too young," and June said, "No, she's not," but Alberto said never mind because it was time to go.

We went to a nearby hotel where you could rent a room for a couple of hours. As June followed Alberto into Room 23, stumbling, groping for the door frame to hold herself up, her eyes half closed, she turned to look at me and she smiled the most pathetic damned smile. Then Luis opened the door to Number 24 and we went in and he closed the door behind us.

The walls of the room were papered in red and the curtains were red and there was a red cover on the bed and a vase of hideous red plastic flowers on a table beside the sink where he washed. On the nightstand, there was magazines like Lucas had sometimes showed me, with pictures of naked women. There was cigarette butts in the waste can and a black seamed stocking that I didn't notice at first, but then we were sitting on the bed and Luis was feeling me up inside my blouse and under my slip and rubbing me between my legs, and I grabbed hold of the pillow. That's when I felt the stocking, so slinky and slippery between my fingers I had to open my eyes to see what it was. Luis looked too, and then he unzipped his fly and wrapped first the stocking and then my fingers around his hard thing and I did what I knew he wanted me to, I pumped him fast and fierce. He looked at me and he said, "You know what you're doing, don't you, Lily?" and I said I did, and he said, *"Con mucho gusto, niña,"* and when he came it spread across the stocking like a silvery mist.

*"Tu también?"* he asked. I knew enough Spanish from what June had brought home and what Alberto had taught me to understand what Luis meant, and to answer him, *"Por favor."* So he made a silky ball of the sticky stocking and he spread me open and pushed it inside me and I rode the ball and his fingers and as I came, good God almighty, as I came the sound of my mother's passion on the other side of the wall made me reel with nausea, but when I tried to throw up in the sink it was just some dry heaves.

The next day June was hungover from too much champagne so she stayed in bed all day. For a while I helped the widow, but I was short-tempered with the children and she told me to do something else. I washed the bathroom floor on my hands and knees with a scrub brush and ammonia that made me gag when I took a breath. Later on I had some supper and watched a drama on television, and every now and then when June called me and told me to bring her a glass of water or some aspirin and once when she asked if I'd rub her head, I felt nauseous the way I had in that hotel room, because her hair was matted with sweat and sick and her forehead was clammy and I could still smell the alcohol on her like it was seeping out of her pores. And when she said I was doing it too hard, I had to stop so I wouldn't tear her hair out and bash her face in, no balance between us now, the fulcrum crumbling beneath us.

It was a couple of anxious and fretful days later; June had gone back to work, when late that afternoon me and the widow were saying good-bye to the last of the children and picking up from their play, and here's Alberto's Lincoln pulling up in front of the house and here's June and Alberto and Luis coming up the walk, June wearing a pair of high-heeled shoes covered in rhinestones and another new hat, Alberto wearing a hat too, Luis bareheaded with a gardenia in his hand that he tucked carefully behind my ear as he kissed me once on each cheek.

I was glad to see him, truth to tell I was crazy excited just to feel how he wanted me, like all it took was the sight of him to convert anxiety to desire. As soon as I got in the car, Luis told June to turn up the radio and while a woman was singing something sad in Spanish, he started telling me how much he loved me, and asking me did I love him too? I wasn't sure if I did or not, but I knew I wanted to, God, how I wanted to, because it would mean we were something together. So I told him I did, and I liked saying it there in the car and when we got to the hotel I said it as we climbed the stairs to the same room and inside that room I gave him the rest of what he wanted.

It was easy. It was *so* easy. We did it on the floor and in front of the mirror above the sink and on the bed, and I found I didn't mind it when he did it to me, but I liked it better when I did it to him. I liked sitting in his lap or squatting above him and making all the moves. It seemed he liked it better too. "You're too good, Lily," he said. "You shouldn't be so good. You're gonna make me come too fast."

"I'm fourteen-and-a-half-years old," I said to him as his eyes rolled back in his head and his back arched.

"You are fourteen and a half?" he asked through his clenched teeth. "Then I'm going to give you something special."

He held me so tight I saw stars, and I could feel him pull himself back from his climax. Then he kissed my face and laid me down on the bed and ate me alive, dropped his mouth down to my sex so fast I didn't have time to let either one of us know my surprise, swallowed me whole and finished me off in no time flat.

And so what if I felt like shit when we finished, that's what I thought later that night and in the morning and after every time I saw Luis, so what if I felt like it was all for nothing, me and him nothing, and June and Alberto nothing, and me and her and Theo and heat and sex and love nothing at all?

The middle of a Wednesday afternoon, hot and steamy inside the widow's house. I'd been sitting outside reading a book to Bessie, and there was shade but no relief under the big acacia tree where me and the little girl had fallen asleep when, "Lily, shhhh," June woke me, pointing to the child in my arms, breathing hard, the smell of tobacco like a haze around her. "There's something going on at the factory," she whispered. Then she knelt beside me and panted as she told me what she knew: She'd been standing at the watercooler when the trouble started back in the office and she could hear furniture knocking against walls and windows breaking. That was enough for her to grab her pocketbook from her locker and make a run for it, though she said she slowed down when she got out onto the street where a man sitting in a parked car with tinted windows called to her, "Hey, *chiquita*," he said, "where are you going in such a hurry? Is somebody after you?" He was dark-skinned like Luis and he had a mustache and a gold tooth. June shook her head and said she was going home to her husband. He nodded and said that was a good reason to hurry.

Now the telephone rang inside the house and the widow called out that it was for June and my mother said for me to wait there. I didn't like the sound of what she'd told me but I didn't know what to make of it and then Bessie woke up crying, hot and sweaty and scared by the sound of an airplane flying low overhead. I was stroking her cheek and trying to lure her into a game of hide-and-seek when June burst out of the house, waving her hands in the air and cursing loud enough to send the child into another crying fit. June was talking too fast and making no sense and Bessie was scream ing like someone was beating her to death. The widow came running out of the house and across the yard. "What is wrong with that girl?" she wailed as she grabbed the child from my arms.

Stunned and confused, I watched June pack while she told me what Alberto had said: him and Luis were both married and married well, to two sisters whose father owned more than a cigar factory, though he did, he owned a few of them and some nightclubs and a piece of the jai alai fronton. He'd sent someone to Alberto's office to straighten things out, but his reach went far beyond Ybor City. He knew our names and where we lived, but he wasn't going to bother us to-night, wasn't even going to bother us in the morning, so we could take our time, just so long as we were gone by sunset the next evening, and Alberto had already wired us some money, we could pick it up at the Western Union office on our way out of town. "Sounds like a goddamned Western, doesn't it?" June snorted as she folded the last of her white dresses and laid them in our biggest suitcase.

I was trying to remember what I was supposed to be doing with my own clothes, still in piles on the bed, but nothing made sense, not the empty suitcase on the floor at my feet, not even my hands at the ends of my arms. "What the hell are you doing?" June snapped as she struggled to close the huge tan valise. "Give me a hand here." She sat down on the top and pointed to the fasteners.

"What about Luis?" I asked, not so much because he was the thing that most concerned me, but because speaking of him was as close as I could come to expressing my horror: it wasn't just that we were leaving again, it was what we'd done that had led up to the leaving, it was what *I* had done, and maybe before I knew it was coming to an end, I hadn't thought about it, but now it was all there before me and upon me and it was almost more than I could bear, how wretched, how far outside of life my life was, and how alone I was in it.

"What about him?" June struggled with the suitcase and when it was closed she looked at me and I could see it coming. "Christ sake, Lily, he's practically a colored." She shook her head with each word like she was throwing it off and all that went with it. "You talk about him like he mattered. He never mattered. We were just using him. But that's okay, 'cause he was just using us too." She stood up and lit a cigarette and leaned against the closet door. "I should have known better than to run around with a bunch of spics. But I'll tell you the truth, if I hadn't heard what went on in the factory, I'd laugh the whole damned thing off because I don't feel like leaving, not one bit."

Well, I didn't want to go either, but I didn't want to stay just as bad. I didn't want to think about what I wanted because nothing felt right, so in the end I packed my bags and helped June load up the trunk of the waiting taxi and I said good-bye to the widow. And when she cried and told me I'd been a good friend to her and the children would miss me, I cried too. I sobbed in her arms and I clung to her neck and when June asked me what the hell I was so choked up about I told her it was none of her goddamned business, she wouldn't understand, forget it. June said she was happy to forget the whole damned place and all the people in it, she wished to hell she could forget me along with the rest, and then she smacked me across the face and I felt my lip split and I smacked her back and I felt her cheekbone hard against my hand and she hit me again and I hit her too and then she hit me with both hands, so many times I lost count. Finally she stopped, she pinned her hands under her arms and I did the same and that's when I realized that as long as I was with June, one way or another I was in danger for my life.

# Chapter 15

I wanted her to die, that's what I wanted. How else was I to be free of her, since as long as she lived, I seemed bound to her still? And, bound to her, how would I survive? What if the next time they didn't call first, or show us the door? What if the next time they came for us? And what if there wasn't even a next time? What if it was just me and her like before, like now: when would the smack turn to a punch or a kick? Because hadn't I seen it, how she held herself back? And what if she didn't, and I didn't either? Never mind that we were matched in strength, no matter who won it would kill me, all of it was killing me, living with it was like dying, and maybe now I knew what Caroline meant, living and dying that close, that's what it had come to.

How it had come to look was June got a fever blister and a sty both at the same time. I sometimes watched her on the bus where she sat brooding in her seat, picking at the one, scratching the other, and kneading her temples with her knuckles to get some relief from a bad headache. Of course, I looked hard up myself, my lip was still sore, the split fresh and tender, and we hadn't slept in a bed more than once or twice since we'd left Florida. We'd been riding day and night for close to a week, like the thing we'd left Tampa to get away from was close as ever. Most times I sat far enough from her so that I could forget she was there—as though I ever could—but when the buses were crowded and we hadn't much choice about our seats, I sat near her as I had to, saying little or nothing, mostly nothing, as afraid of my own rage as I was of hers.

I talked instead to the other passengers when I found a lady I could persuade to set down her book or a man who didn't mind so much if I kept him from his nap or from watching the scenery go by. I was sometimes even insistent, I could hear it in my voice, the desperation, and maybe they heard it too, and that was why, even though before I'd always had company and invites when I'd wanted them, now suddenly company was hard-won and invites never came, when they were just the thing I was desperate for. Something to come between me and my mother, a game of cards, a good story—better yet, a place to spend the night, just me and not her, and they'd like me so much they'd ask me to stay on. And then it would be time for school and they'd take me down and register me in the eighth grade, and where it said on the form to put your last name they'd write theirs and that's when I'd see the light, right there where we were standing with the lady behind the tall desk who wore her cardigan over her shoulders and buttoned at the neck to keep it from falling off, that's when the light would come like God Himself had come down to bless me in my new life, because that's what I needed, a whole new life, and I needed it bad, I really couldn't wait.

We were waiting one afternoon for our bus to Memphis to pull out of Tupelo and I was jumping out of my skin, chewing my fingernails and grinding my teeth. But everybody was on edge, June and the other passengers and the driver alike. It had been raining hard all day, the kind of rain that gives no relief, that doesn't clear the air but only adds a load to it. There was no ice left for cold drinks at the lunch counter in the station, and the air-conditioning on the bus was busted.

My seat was about halfway to the back, the seat beside me empty now, the boy from Hattiesburg who'd told me I talked too much had got off in Meridian. June was across the aisle, and only a couple of seats behind her was a white lady who had two little babies with her, both boys, and dressed identically in yellow-and-blue rompers like they were twins except one was white and one was colored. That in itself would have made serious trouble on the most temperate day of the year. But ninety-seven degrees and midday skies nearly dark as night had ravaged those babies and they were setting up a serious protest.

I watched from my window as the driver ran across the parking lot, dodging the puddles and missing no fewer than he hit. He climbed the bus steps, wiped his wet face on his wet arm, and took his seat. And as he turned the key, he looked in the direction of the howling. Then he turned off the engine, got up from his seat, and walked back to where the lady and her babies were taking up, it's true, two seats for the price of one, although it really didn't make a hell of a lot of difference, since there was at least a half-dozen empty seats.

Right there in the aisle, a couple of rows in front of the lady and her little boys, the driver stopped and said, "You got to shut those children up." His voice was composed, though you could see it was costing him something to speak that way. But then he took those last couple of steps and all of a sudden his composure was gone. "What the hell do you have there? Have you got a colored baby halfway to the front of this bus? It ain't enough you ought to have paid for both the seats you're occupying, you got to be setting there with a colored baby in a seat for whites only."

"That ain't the law no more," the lady hollered above the little boys' crying.

"Lady, this is my bus," the driver roared, "and on my bus, I'm the law." Then he told her to get her things together and move herself and the both of those kids to the rear of the bus, which is where they should have been all along, and she'd better make it fast, because he was not leaving the station until she did it, and he wasn't planning on being late for the next stop.

That's when a squeaky-voiced colored girl stepped up from the shadows. "I'll quiet those babies," she said. "I got some vanilla bean for 'em to suck on. Give 'em here." She pointed to the babies with the index finger of her small right hand, that's all she did, but that simple gesture sent something through me that made me tremble in my seat.

The bus driver was not trembling. "They can suck on your handbag, for all I care," he said. "That ain't my problem. But they ain't doing it anywhere except the back of this bus."

"It's too hot to put those children back there," the girl said. "You want quiet, you let 'em stay where they are and have a taste of the bean."

"Now I got another problem," the driver said. "Now I want *you* quiet."

She looked at the driver and then she looked at the floor and then she looked at the driver again. It was my guess that she'd have looked back at the floor and then she probably would've moved on back to her seat and I'd have joined her, but she didn't get the chance so neither did I. A crackling clap of thunder rattled the bus and the babies' screams reached a fever pitch. The lady was scrambling for her things and the girl moved to help her and the driver grabbed ahold of the girl's shoulder with his one hand and jerked her away and then he smacked her across the face with the other. Me and June looked at each other like we'd just seen a ghost and then everybody on the bus, me and my mother and the babies included, stopped breathing, as though something had taken possession of our lungs that also made our eyes bulge and our mouths hang open, everybody's mouth, that is, except for the girl's, which was clenched shut like a stitched-up slit across her face, as the brown skin of her cheek turned a deep persimmon color.

"Don't you dare hit that girl again," the lady said, the little boys clutched to her chest.

"I can take care of myself," the girl said and she made to turn toward the back of the bus.

"You got a bag?" the driver said.

"I got a small valise," the girl answered.

"Get it and get off," the driver said.

Me and June spoke at the same time. "Don't you say a thing," she said to me.

"She doesn't have to get off the goddamned bus," I said to the driver and I stepped one foot out into the aisle.

Then everybody had something to say. The babies started crying again, but there was so much shouting that you could hardly hear them. Another crash of thunder clapped the sky and then the rain let loose in earnest. The colored girl inched past me, holding her suitcase in front of her like a shield. The driver turned his back to her, led her to the front of the bus, and watched her walk down the stairs, and I followed, sure and certain that my waiting was over.

"Where the hell are you going?" I could hear my mother shriek above the commotion. By then I was already crossing the parking lot, glad I was too far away to answer because the truth was I didn't know where I was going, but it wasn't my usual notion of destination that had my pulse racing, it was destiny.

I stood beside the colored girl under the overhang to one side of the station. She was at least ten years older than me, probably closer to June's age than mine, short and skinny, and she had Chinese eyes and pickaninny plaits bound at the ends with red cotton twine. "You better get back on that bus," she said. "He won't wait for you." She touched her cheek with the back of her hand and made a gruff sound deep in her throat.

"Where are you going?" I asked her—it must have been like a nervous twitch, my asking her that.

"What's it to you?" she came back at me, but I didn't have to answer, because here came June, down the steps of the bus and the driver right behind her, to unlock the baggage compartment and dig our suitcases out and drop them in the mud.

The driver was already back in his seat and shifting into gear as June dragged a bag to where me and the colored girl were standing, and the three of us watched the bus pull onto the road. I dragged another bag over just as the lights went dark inside the station and a man in a pair of greasy overalls came out and locked the door behind him. "The pay phone works," he said, pointing to a telephone booth I could just about see through the rain, about a hundred yards beyond the parking lot. "You got to hit it hard after you put your dime in, but it works." He made a gesture with the heel of his hand to show us what he meant and then he got into a flatbed pickup and drove off.

"Who do you think we ought to call?" June said. "I know," she went on, "why don't you call your daddy, or better yet, your grandmother. Tell her we're stuck here in this shitty little town with about seven dollars in our pockets . . ."

I looked at her to see if she was shamming about our money—her hair was wet and stringy, some of it stuck to her face like flatworms, and her eyes were bloodshot, but she didn't look like she was lying. She fished out a cigarette from her purse and struck a match, took a long drag, and popped the smoke out in a set of perfect rings. Then she looked at me. "That's right," she said, "seven dollars, that's what we got left."

Shit, I thought to myself, because even I knew seven dollars was close to broke. But we'd been broke before and there were other matters that concerned me now. "I got a pocketful of change," I said, mostly stalling for time.

"You got another cigarette?" the colored girl asked June. June handed her the pack and the girl helped herself.

"You got a dime?" the girl asked.

"I got a dime," I said, and I pulled one from my pocket and offered it to her.

"It's a good thing for you that my girl is such a chump," June said with a sneer. "I know better. I mean, why the hell would I give you a dime?"

The girl took the coin from me, flipped it in the air, and smacked it down on the back of her other hand. "You'd give me a dime," she said to June, "because I got somebody close by on the other end of the line and you don't."

"Who you've got doesn't mean a damned thing to me," June said.

"Suit yourself," the girl said. Then she looked at me and she said, "Call it."

"Heads," I said. And then I asked her was she traveling without any money, because if she was, I was thinking maybe we could, and then I corrected myself, maybe I could.

"I'm traveling with plenty of money," the girl said. "But I don't like to carry around a lot of change. It weighs me down." She winked at me with one of her Chinese eyes and she lifted her hand so we could both see the dime, the head showing, and she smiled. Then her smile disappeared and she turned to June. "Just to save you the trouble, I got my money in my shoe," she said, and then she stepped out from under the overhang and let the rain fall right down on her. "You can have whatever you want from my valise," she added.

Me and June watched her walk toward the phone booth. June finished her cigarette and flicked the butt into a puddle. Then she turned to speak to me, her voice pure venom. "There's not much you could say on any subject that would interest me, but I *would* like to hear what you had in your mind when you followed a goddamned negro girl off the bus. Just tell me that, because I know I'll feel a lot better if I can make some sense of why I'm standing here in this hellhole in the rain." She tapped her toe on the wet cement as she went on about how she'd had something lined up where we were going, a job, a place to stay for a few weeks, a nice place, a pink stucco house with a swimming pool, which I knew was a load of bullshit, but I did not open my mouth or even think to.

"You giving that child the devil?" the colored girl shouted above the din of the rain from halfway across the parking lot. "You ought to be praising her to God and all His angels." She ducked in beside us. There was raindrops like glass beads in her hair and on her eyelashes.

"Is there a hotel in this town?" I asked, because if she was staying on, so was I.

"There's a place they call a hotel," the girl said. "Most of the guests are rats and cockroaches. But they don't pay."

"What's the next biggest town?" June asked.

"Columbus," the girl answered.

"We already been to Columbus," June said.

"By the looks of you, you've been everywhere," the girl said, and then she laughed, so full in her laughter, with her arms wrapped around herself and her head nodding with each chortle of pleasure. We did look like we'd been everywhere. June's skirt was torn and stained, and the hem was brown. Her skin was a real mess too, red blotches and angry swells on her forehead and at either side of her nose. I looked just as bad, half a shoelace in each shoe, a big gash on my ankle from when I'd walked into the corner of a bed in the rooming house where we'd stayed a few nights before. And I'd grown out of the pants I was wearing, they were short and tight and so was my blouse, tight and missing a button. The girl was right.

I guess June thought so too because she looked us over, me and her, and then she started to come around, though what really brought her to was the jar of hooch the colored girl pulled from the pocket of her skirt. She took a long swallow and held it out to my mother, whose mouth twitched at the corners and then she bit her cheek, took the jar, smelled it, put it to her lips and drank slow, passed the jar back to the girl and said, "Thanks. I needed that."

"I didn't catch your names," the girl said.

"I'm Lily Wolsey," I said so fast my tongue about tripped over my teeth.

"I'm June," my mother said.

"I'd like another one of your cigarettes," the girl said. "Oh, and my name's Ada Crears."

Ada was just taking a light from the match June held to her cigarette when a car pulled into the lot, a brand-new black Cadillac, all fins and fandangles, the windshield wipers switching back and forth making a blur of the man behind the wheel. "Here's my fella. He'll run us up to Memphis," she said.

The Cadillac stopped right in front of us and a big colored man in a straw hat and a shiny black slicker eased himself slowly out of the driver's seat, rain pounding the brim of his hat and his huge back like pebbles flying off a stony face of the Blue Ridge Mountains. He gathered up our bags, Ada's of course, and then he looked at her and she nodded so he got June's and mine too and he set them all in the trunk. Then he opened the doors and smiled—he had crooked teeth and green eyes pale and fiery—and the three of us dashed into the car, Ada in the front seat beside him, me and June in the back.

June looked around, I figured it was to see if somebody was watching us, a white woman and a white girl, getting into a car with two colored, and I was already hating her all over again for caring, but just as I was closing the door, somebody rattled open a window across the street and shouted "nigger lovers." June turned the collar up on her blouse like it was something to hide behind. Ada lowered her window fast and spit a good ten feet in the direction of the voice and then she rolled the window up and made the introductions like nothing had happened.

The man's name was High Pockets and he nodded his hellos, touched Ada's wet hair with a hand big as a catcher's mitt, put his fat fingers to her lips and let her kiss settle him in his seat so he sank a good half foot as he rolled that lumbering car onto the highway. Right away Ada told High Pockets about what happened on the bus and the two of them laughed about it and I laughed too. I wished I had something to say so they could see how clever and funny I was, but I couldn't think of a thing and my silence made me agitated. But pretty soon the rain stopped and the air cleared and there was a nice breeze coming in the open windows. Ada and June smoked the last of June's cigarettes and when they finished hers, High Pockets stopped and bought some more. He whistled and sang a lot of the time, sang softly, just the tune, no words. June sat deep into the corner of the backseat behind High Pockets, looking out the window at the countryside, sometimes looking over at me. I sat easy now, in the corner behind Ada, wondering why I felt so safe riding in a car with a colored man driving and a colored girl rubbing the back of his neck, especially because I was noticing signs painted on the sides of barns, BURN THE NIGGERS, NIGGERS DIE, like I'd never seen such things before, which of course I had, but you better believe they looked different from the backseat of that Cadillac.

Just the same, it wasn't much of a drive, and when we got to Memphis at about six o'clock and High Pockets said we ought to have something to eat, I said I sure was hungry, but June said for him not to bother, we'd grab a bite around the bus station if he'd just drop us off near there. Ada nudged High Pockets with her elbow and he said, "Huh?" to her and then he said, "Oh," and then he said to me and June they'd take it personal if we wouldn't be their guests at a barbecue place where they served the finest pulled pork in Memphis. I said I loved pulled pork even though I couldn't imagine what it was, and June said no thank you, but then Ada dug the jar from her pocket and offered it to June and said there was more of it, plenty more, and a far better quality brew at the barbecue. June took the jar and said all right and Ada nodded at me and I nodded back.

We had our dinner at a big table covered with an oilcloth and before we were done we all had barbecue gravy on our fingers and chins and spills of it in front of us, so it looked like we'd forgotten about forks and knives and napkins. June was the worst of the lot of us, less for the food than the punch they served in white enameled cups, drinking like a fugitive. All the while she was looking around at the small room crowded with colored people, laughing loud and joking. Among them was one other white woman my mother could not take her eyes off. She was all dressed up in a red feather hat, laughing and joking loud as the rest. High Pockets said hello to her in a voice part grit and gravel, part honey and molasses, called her Dolly so it sounded like it was her name, and she called him Hollander and jutted her chin at him with her mouth in a pretty little pout. Ada hissed just like a cat—and I felt the hair on the back of my neck stand up like I was a cat too—and High Pockets slapped his hat on his knee and whooped out loud. You could see his green eyes shining, you could see his big pink tongue flapping inside his mouth. I could. I did. His voice and his eyes and his tongue, and the snaky black curls of his long hair played on me like a bow on a fiddle.

A girl in a yellow-checked apron with a matching ribbon in her hair came to clear the table and wipe down the oilcloth and I got up to use the ladies' room. "Ain't got but one," Ada warned me.

"What do you mean?" I asked.

"Ain't got no white and colored rest rooms here," she said. "You got to use ours."

"It's all the same to Lily," June said, kind of nasty.

"What of it?" I spat at her.

"All the same to me too," Ada said.

"And that's nice," High Pockets said, "that's real nice, that's the way it ought to be."

"That's a load of crap," June said as she followed me across the dining room to the ladies' room. We had it to ourselves and after I peed, I washed my face and hands and watched her looking into the mirror. "What's next, Lily?" she said. "What you got lined up for us now?"

I dried my hands on the damp roller towel that hung from the wall beside the sink. "Here we are in Memphis, just like you planned, pink stucco house, isn't that what you said?" I didn't wait for her to answer, I left her there and made my way back to the table and my new future.

For dessert we ate some peach pie. I was halfway through a second slice when June crossed the room and sat down. She said no thank you when High Pockets offered her pie and coffee and then Ada paid the check from the roll of bills she took out of her shoe—a gesture not wasted on my mother.

When we climbed back into the Caddy, June said for High Pockets to drop us off anywhere downtown and we'd find ourselves a room. That was the last thing I wanted to happen but I had a feeling if I kept my mouth shut, it wouldn't, and then, like he was dedicated to making me right, High Pockets looked at Ada and then he said he wouldn't hear of it, not at that hour, Memphis was no place for a couple of unescorted women to be walking the streets at night looking for a hotel. I said I'd heard that about Memphis and thanked him for his kindness and consideration. June didn't even look at me, though I could see her jaw clench when she asked Ada if there was anything left in the jar.

An old, run-down frame house is where we ended up that night. We followed a cracked and broken stretch of sidewalk from the street, across a yard with patches of brown grass here and there, to a front porch in an uncertain relationship to the rest of the house. Ada warned us about the porch, said they didn't have the money to fix it but it did its job just the same, hung the black sign she pointed to as if we hadn't already seen it, as if we could miss it, ANTONIA'S painted in big red letters.

"Who's Antonia?" June asked.

"A white lady who used to own the place," Ada answered.

"Who owns it now?" I asked.

"Me," Ada said.

"What is it?" June asked.

"Have a look inside," High Pockets said.

I had the feeling it was a bar before I even stepped through the door from the music coming through the open windows, and then once I was inside I knew for sure from the smell of liquor and the lights so low. Ada said to leave our bags in the hall and she'd show us around.

There was a white man and a colored man playing cards by the light of a kerosene lamp at a table in what I figured used to be the dining room on account of the empty china closet. Both the men were wearing straw porkpie hats and the colored man was wearing dark glasses and chewing a toothpick. Ada said good evening to them and promised the winner a drink on the house and they tipped their hats at her.

The kitchen was even darker than the hall and the dining room, just one vanity-table lamp with a pleated pink shade set on a chair, no overhead fixture and no kitchen table, empty cases of pop and beer bottles stacked on top of the range and beside the refrigerator, ragged curtains hanging at odd angles from the windows and the back door.

The barroom was dark too, heavy black curtains covered the parlor windows, and bare bulbs, red, green, blue, and gold, hung low from the ceiling, mostly above the bar itself, with a couple in the corners. The jukebox, the brightest thing in the room, was between records when we walked in, and a colored couple was standing in the middle of the floor waiting for the next number.

Ada said hello to the handsome, light-skinned colored man standing behind the bar. He was talking to a heavyset negro who reached his arm toward Ada, but she pulled back from his reach. " 'Evening, Andrew," Ada said, cool, cold, right out of the icebox. Then High Pockets came up and put his arm around the man's shoulder, raised his glass to us, and over the song from the jukebox came his honey voice, "To your health, ladies."

I could get a better look at High Pockets now: big, baggy pants, too short by several inches, wide at the waist to match his pear shape and hanging from a pair of suspenders that crisscrossed in the back where his fleshy sides tugged at his shirt. Giant High Pockets, his smile, his pear shape, his suspenders, all of it made my heart swell in my throat and stick there, a hunger too big to swallow.

Ada asked if we wanted to have a drink and June said she was spent but she wouldn't mind a nightcap, which the bartender poured and June downed in one quick swig. Then Ada gave us a hand with our bags and showed us the upstairs, the bathroom and three bedrooms: one of them filled with furniture piled to the ceiling, chairs and a sofa and floor lamps and a bed and dresser; one of them Ada's; and one of them the guest room—ours, at least for the night.

" 'Scuse me for not turning down the sheets," she said with a grin. "Just so's you'll know, there idn't a thing to eat around here, so if you wake up early and hungry, you got to satisfy yourselves with pork rinds and chips from behind the bar," and she closed the door on her way out.

I sat down on our bed and the springs creaked and groaned. June stretched out on the far side. "Lumpiest bed I ever laid down on," she said.

I ran my hand across the dimpled mattress. "Once you fall asleep you won't feel it," I said. "It sure as hell isn't any worse than most of the beds you've slept on. Not near as bad as the seat of a bus."

"How am I going to sleep with that music downstairs?" June sat up. "What on earth are we doing here?" she asked me, *she* asked *me*.

"Here where?" I asked, playing with her.

"Here in this house or this bar or whatever the hell it is.

Colored bar, for Christ sake, you and me pale as the sheets of the men who cook colored for sport."

"One of the men at the card table was white and the bartender was fair-skinned," I played some more, loving it.

"High yellow, that's what they call it. A quadroon most probably, quarter negro, but negro just the same." She stalked the room looking for an ashtray, found one on the windowsill, lit a cigarette. "What the hell is it with you and colored?" she said and she pulled the sheer curtain back and stared out at the street.

I didn't answer because I didn't know the answer and I didn't feel like making something up and I didn't feel like I had to. I came up next to her, took her cigarette from the ashtray, drew in cautiously and let the smoke make my brains sway inside my head.

June took the cigarette from me and set it back in the ashtray. "Oh well, I don't guess anything's going to happen this one night," she said, "and come morning we can find ourselves other accommodations."

But come morning, High Pockets woke us up, banging on our door and saying for us to hurry and dress, he wanted to take us all out to breakfast before he headed back to Mississippi. The room was hot and it was late, nearly noon is what I figured from the sun so high. Me and June were tangled in the sheets like we'd been tied to the bed or each other or both. I hollered to High Pockets that we'd be dressed in a minute. "Like hell we will," June said as she tugged at the sheets.

"Suit yourself," I said, and I leaped up from the bed and into an odd assortment of clothes cleaner than the ones I'd had on the day before.

"Are those my capri pants you're wearing?" June asked me as we climbed into the backseat of the Cadillac.

"Uh-huh," is all I said.

We had steak and eggs at a lady's house; like the bar, it wasn't exactly a restaurant, but you paid them for what they fed you. All the other customers were colored, but me and June being white didn't seem of any particular interest to them or the man who took our order and served us plates of scrambled eggs and tough, juicy strips of steak and stacks of toast with apricot preserves.

I guess while we were still asleep Ada had been to the hairdresser. Her twine-bound plaits were gone now and her hair was sculpted in all kinds of fancy waves that looked as though the sea had printed itself on her head, and she was wearing a black suit, a tight straight skirt with a high kick pleat and a jacket with pearl buttons. I asked why she was all fixed up and she said it was to go see a man about some financial matters. The man was High Pockets' boss, the Mississippi white man whose car he drove and who sometimes made business loans to colored people. What would she do with the money? I asked. She said she wanted to fix up Antonia's, get the porch repaired, fresh coats of paint inside and out, some new lamps and tables and chairs, some booths for the barroom, and plates and silverware so she could serve meals too. Then she talked about the things I didn't understand, this many thousands of dollars, interest rates, payment schedules, so I just sat and listened, while June, I know, was counting it all up like an adding machine. She chimed in with an opinion from time to time like she knew what she was talking about, which it turned out she did because that's what High Pockets said, "Sounds like you know what you're talking about, Miss June," he said, and then he asked the man to bring us more toast and coffee and more tea for the two ladies.

"How many sugars you like?" I asked him as he lifted his spoon.

"Two heaping sugars," he said, "that's what it takes."

Ada turned to me and raised an eyebrow. "Two sugars ought to be enough for any man," she said, and I knew she wasn't talking about tea, which was fine with me because neither was I. Then she asked for the check and she paid again. "Drive me over to Mr. Oliver's hotel and then take Lily and June back to the house," she said. "I'll get a cab home later on."

Back at Antonia's High Pockets opened the door with a key he handed to June on the porch. "Delivery man usually come on Wednesday with Ada's beer order. He know where to put it. I got to go back to Tupelo. I be back late Friday. Hope you two still around."

As soon as he was gone, June said she didn't mean to see High Pockets again, but she did want to clean herself up before we moved on, so she was soaking in the bathtub when the delivery came. The driver switched his full cases for Ada's empties, and then he sat beside me on the front porch and drank a warm beer, offered me the last swallow from his bottle after he wiped the glass with his clean handkerchief, didn't take offense when I said no thank you, wiped the sweat off his blond brow with the back of his hand. "Hot day, ain't it?" He drained the last of the beer, squinted at the sun, at me, at the sun, rolled the empty bottle around in his hand. "You know, you could just about pass," he said.

"You think so?" I asked him, and I smiled modestly.

"No doubt about it," he replied.

After he left, after he drove off in his delivery truck, empty bottles rattling down the street, I was looking close at my arm, looking for colored in my skin, fearing it, wishing for it, wondering what on earth it was like to have dark skin and what did it mean, and finally knowing that it didn't *mean* anything, and that's when June came out onto the porch and sat down beside me. My mother had incredible powers of recovery. Her hair was wet and slick and her face was clean, the red splotches were already fading from her nose and chin and the sty and the fever blister were healing nicely too, and if her white blouse needed ironing, she looked good just the same. She lit a cigarette and towel-dried her hair. "I'm going to run upstairs and get my comb. I want you to comb my hair out," she said, making nice—at this point, telling me what she wanted me to do was as nice as she got. Then from the doorway she said, "Who was that sitting here beside you?"—her voice surly, her mouth twisted and harsh, every trace of nice gone.

"Go get your comb," I said because I didn't need her nice.

I was working out the knots in June's hair when a taxi dropped Ada off in front of the house. "Have a seat," I said to her, like she was my guest, and she said thank you like being my guest was fine with her, and then she sat down, not there on the stoop but on a canvas camp stool she brought from just inside the front door, crossed her legs so you could hear her stockings slide against each other, unbuttoned her suit jacket, picked at her teeth with a matchstick she took from her jacket pocket.

"How did your meeting go?" June asked.

"I didn't get the money," she said after a while. "I got a note, though, a note of promise. What the hell does that mean?"

June took the comb from me. "Means you're wasting your time," she said.

"I hate to think you're right," Ada said.

"I know how you feel," June said.

"I'd sure like the cash," Ada said.

"How much did you ask him for?" I asked.

Ada looked at June and smiled. "Fifteen thousand dollars," she said, and then she laughed. "Look at your eyes, girl. Turning green as Lily's. You got a real love of money, don't you?"

"The more I don't have it, the more I love it," June said.

"You stick around and it comes to me, I might throw a little your way," Ada said as she scraped at the tip of the matchstick with her thumbnail.

"Stick around here?" I asked, because I could hardly believe my ears, it was too close to the very thing I wanted to hear.

June said, "What kind of place is this for us?"

"A place to get rich," Ada said.

My mother pointed to the houses up and down the street. Most of them were in need of paint and repairs to sagging roofs and busted windowpanes, and the yards were choked with broken furniture and sodden cardboard boxes. A lot of the cars parked at the curb were truly beat-up—dented hoods, fenders lashed to frames with lengths of rope, doors hung at funny angles. "Seems to me money is beside the point on this block," June said.

"On this block, money is exactly the point," Ada said as she came to sit beside my mother on the stoop. "See here, most colored in this town plays checkers or dice, but that's poor folks' play. Me and High Pockets want to have a card game. Won't nobody bother to make a fuss about a card game on this block except the few people I'd like to, and I got the notion the minute I laid eyes on you way back yesterday afternoon, how a white woman dealing cards might be a curious attraction to those very same few. More recently this morning, I also got the notion you can count to five or seven or however many cards a hand requires and I'll teach you the rest. You and Lily can have that room to yourselves, have your meals too, as soon as we get the kitchen going, and a modest amount of liquor. And I'll pay you good. I like to pay my help good, specially my white help. The only relations between white and negro I trust is when there's money changing hands." She shot me a glance like she wanted me to know that I was somehow spared this judgment and then she looked back at June with a firmness that made you doubt she'd ever looked away. "Somehow, I suspect that suits you too, even if what you're used to is seeing it pass from white to colored."

I took the comb back from June, turned it over in my hand and tugged at the long strands of her hair caught in the teeth. "As long as she gets her share of it, June doesn't give a damn which way it passes."

"Hot dog," Ada said, and she looked at me with new respect.

My mother held her face real still for an instant, and then she broke into a wary smile, like she wasn't sure whether or not she thought what I'd said suited her. "Oh, yeah," she said, "that Lily's a real hot dog, all right."

# *Chapter 16*

There was no further mention of wieners. June said yes and I
said yes and Ada said yes and when High Pockets telephoned
that night, he said yes too. We were such an agreeable bunch,
everybody was so satisfied with this arrangement, except for
June because she said in private to me that if Tampa had
taught her anything it was to avoid unsavory business associations, but things being what they were, we didn't really have
much choice. And also except for me, because I didn't like
how Ada's plan not only included June, it featured her, but I
figured I could live with it while I was putting into effect a
plan of my own that featured me and Ada and High Pockets
exclusively.

Just how exclusive did I have in mind? You figure it out: I
was in love.

I was in love, but it split me in two. My weekday love was
for her, my weekend love was for him. Monday through Friday I wanted only one thing, to be her, or else to be like her,
saucy, bold, and I tried to walk like her and talk like her,

and when June said Ada's walk looked silly and Ada's talk sounded dumb on a little white girl, I said I wasn't little and June said okay, she'd give me that much, but what about the rest? And I said to hell with the rest.

But come Friday night all my love was for that man, High Pockets, Hollander, whatever his name was—I called him Honey to myself and then I had him answer me with kisses and praise and song. Mind you, he wasn't that taken with me, or he was, but it didn't bother him, didn't make him flustered or wear him down like it did me. Oh, he liked me all right, I suspect he even enjoyed my infatuation, and the way my eyes followed his every move. I think he knew how I felt when he was near, and if he didn't share my longing, then I think he appreciated it.

So he left things around—a glove, a penknife, a package of jelly beans—where he knew I'd find them, that's what I thought, so I could turn them over and look at them and feel him close just for having them with me. He made stupid jokes that nobody laughed at but him and me. He'd call out my name in the middle of a sentence so everybody turned to stare at me like I was the crazy one, and I guess I was: once he told me to come with him and Ada for a walk to the candy store and she said, "Fine idea," but when he kissed her in front of the licorice jar, I believed the kiss was for me and the way he looked at her when he drew back from that kiss and let his hand dangle from her shoulder, that was for me too.

June said I was making a perfect ass of myself. I said I didn't care. And anyway, I said, a perfect ass might be the very thing to interest a man like him. "Damn it to hell, Lily," she said, "seems to me you like them just because they're colored. But I'm warning you, don't you get yourself tied up with them, they're slow and they're lazy and they're dirty, but worse than that, they got some nasty habits, not the least of which is getting their heads kicked in by whites, and I'm telling you, girl, if you're standing too close when the kicking begins, you're going to feel those boots too."

In the first place, I didn't so much *like* them because they were colored as I didn't *not* like them because they were colored. And then there was this too—that I was supposed to not like them for that very reason, it was how she'd always wanted me to be, but race was one thing I'd never felt I had to give in on, maybe because holding out on their account had always been the same as holding out something of myself for me. And now them and me together seemed like the best shot I had at saving myself from what I feared most—June.

In the second place, I didn't trust the way she talked, like she was just looking out for me. As it turned out, maybe she was right, but you'd have had a hard time convincing me of that back then. Given the ways she hadn't bothered all along.

And about the slow, lazy, dirty part: Ada certainly might have been, plenty of people are, white the same as colored. But she wasn't. She mopped the floors and washed the windows, did business with colored and white all at breakneck speed; always knew how much bourbon and brandy she had behind the bar and downstairs in the cellar; answered the phone and knew the voice of every caller.

I knew these things because I was forever at her side, learning her ways as fast as I could. Too fast is what Ada said— "What's your hurry, girl? Who you got at your back?" I didn't tell her, "June," I didn't tell her anything, though I think she suspected it for how she came between me and my mother whenever she could, taking my side in our spats, providing June with as much liquor as she wanted when she wasn't dealing cards. "Your mama like to be high," Ada said. "I like her that way myself. She's a happy drunk, best kind there is, and when it don't make her happy it make her sleep."

And Ada's hard work wasn't for nothing—it seemed like in

no time flat she had herself a going enterprise; fresh faces every night, new friends High Pockets brought around, old friends too, her pastor, her doctor, some of the Beale Street crowd, a few white visitors, but mostly every shade of colored, including an albino card shark from Picayune.

It didn't hurt any—even Ada said so—that June took to dealing like she'd been born to it, learned everything Ada had to teach her like she was just reviewing something she already knew, which it turned out was true to some degree, because she'd learned a lot from Torrence Younger, far more than she'd ever let on, and then she picked up a few tricks from the customers too, who mostly liked to win the game, but sometimes just liked the company of the fair-skinned lady from Virginia who dressed head to toe in white and took to calling her customers animal names, Puppy and Tiger and Chick and Duckie—I saw some of them, and the names mostly fit.

One man she called Turkey right to his face, and she told him to quit the game, he was a born loser. But he came back like her contempt was the best thing that ever happened to him, paid his losses with crisp fresh dollar bills he kept wrapped in a clean white linen napkin, handed June his money, including one fresh dollar for her, with a cluck and a smile and June said, "Gobble, gobble."

And right from the start there was more than just Turkey's dollars. Some couldn't give her but small change but she took it all, from the Tigers and the Duckies and from High Pockets' white boss from Mississippi, Mr. Oliver himself. That first weekend High Pockets brought him to the house for a few hands of poker, him and another white man and two colored, all of them wearing pinkie rings and big hats, turning up their jacket collars against the first chilly nights of autumn, drinking hot coffee and shots of whiskey and tipping June quite generously. On the second Saturday night Mr.

Oliver even gave her a gift, some fancy French perfume in a glass bottle with an elegant cone-shaped stopper, but June said the smell wasn't nearly as fragrant as cash. She put some behind my ears and at my wrists and sniffed at me—"Sweet as a room deodorizer," she said.

The other white man gave her some French money. "It's Marie Antoinette," June said, handing me the French bill and pointing to the picture of a lady with a topple of curls and a low-cut dress.

"Who's she?" I asked.

"A woman greedy as me," June answered.

She slept late most days, tired from the long nights of work, sleeping off the applejack Ada poured her when the last hand was played and won. She'd get up around noon or one o'clock and sometimes on a weekday when I was out running errands with Ada, she'd go to a matinee downtown, or else she'd go shopping in Levy's and Helen's of Memphis, and she'd try on fur coats and diamond rings, which she said she knew she wasn't rich enough to buy yet, but she was seeing enough money pass through her hands to be getting ready for furs and jewels and leaving town, and I thought to myself when? When will she go? though I didn't say it to her.

The truth is, I didn't tell her most of what I was thinking, and that seemed okay with June, she didn't tell me much either. Maybe two people are allotted a certain number of words to say to each other in a lifetime. It's bound to be a lot, a hundred million, two hundred million, but me and her had all but spent our allotment on being hateful and making up, only to be hateful all over again.

A couple of times I did meet her around five o'clock and we sat at the Rexall lunch counter over a couple of chocolate malteds, sometimes I'd have a strawberry milk shake—after all that time, it turned out I didn't much care for chocolate. Then we'd catch a bus home or if June was feeling good, which means wealthy, we'd take a cab. Back at the house, she'd do her nails, lie down, smoke cigarettes in the dark— the curtains drawn and the shades closed—and she'd tell me to wake her around seven. I'd play dominoes or checkers with Kingman Brown, the high-yellow bartender, and then come seven I'd wake her up, bring her the glass of Coca-Cola she said she needed to get herself going.

Ada Crears didn't need the Coke. Mr. Oliver gave her $2,000 of the $15,000 she'd asked for. She said it seemed like a pitiful sum, but she didn't let that stop her, and it wasn't long before the painters finished and she'd filled the cupboards with the glasses, china, and silver she'd bought off a man whose place in Bolivar went bust. The painters and the man from Bolivar took a few dollars in cash and a tab at the bar for their goods and services, so even with less of Mr. Oliver's money than she'd counted on, Ada was making a go of it. She hired a cook, who drank up every penny he made serving po' boy sandwiches and chicken gumbo and then quit on a Saturday night. She hired another cook, a deaf man who fried catfish and walleyes and quit ten days later. As a matter of fact, none of the cooks stayed more than a week, couple weeks tops, but just so long as there was somebody who could satisfy her customers' hunger, somebody who didn't steal from her pantry, the frequent comings and goings didn't matter to Ada.

And it didn't matter that she was up each night till after June had gone to bed. Most mornings, we'd have breakfast together, hot sassafras tea and oatmeal and sliced bananas. She'd tell me stories about her life and what she'd learned: If you wanted to survive being colored in the southern United States, you had to know how to have a good time, because the bad times knew too well how to have you; you had to dance and sing like your life depended on it, because it did; you had to choose your friends, but even more important, you had to choose your enemies, and not everyone you hated or even everyone who hated you was a worthy enemy. For example, the bus driver in Tupelo, he wasn't troublesome enough. A man like that had a long way to go before he could have Ada for a enemy. "And sometimes," she emphasized, "you got to learn to live with your enemies like they was your friends. That man Andrew—"

"He was at the bar the first night we came here? Yellow eyes and losing his hair, that one?"

"That's him. High Pockets's brother. Evil man. And High Pockets know it too, but he won't throw him out, because he's kin. Got a hold on High Pockets like the devil hisself. But it ain't up to me to break his hold. All I can do is watch it. And give him a wide berth. You do the same."

"What makes him evil?" I asked.

"I can't tell you that, but it's a good question," she said. "Fine question. Best kind of question there is. You got to love the questions you can't answer."

She said she bet there were a few questions like that about my own life. I said there wasn't much, but she said hogwash and then she listened while I'd told her everything I've already said to you—and through the best and the worst of it, all she did was nod her head or hum a sound that meant she was glad or she was sorry.

When I was through, she asked me had I ever noticed how it seemed like most of my friends were my enemies too? I said I hadn't paid it any mind, but that didn't mean I couldn't see she was right. Then I changed the subject, it made me feel nervous to talk about it, in part because I thought everybody hated and feared the people they most loved, but also because there was something else I wanted to get to.

What about High Pockets, what did he do in Tupelo? I asked her, trying to make it sound casual, like my life didn't depend on it. She told me how he worked for Mr. Oliver, drove him around in that big black Cadillac, fetched his shirts from the laundress, sat in his kitchen and shined his shoes while the white man with the big droopy pouches under his eyes met with all types of wheelers and dealers on the other side of the parlor door. Then, as if the thought of the man in the seersucker suit and the string tie was pure irritant, she sneezed, loud, very loud.

"That's the loudest sneeze I ever heard," I said.

"Why not? What am I saving it for? Sneeze loud, yawn loud, laugh loud, snore loud too."

"You snore?"

"Me, uh-huh, High Pockets is the same. You mean you can't hear him in your room? He snores so loud I have to snore louder just to keep him from waking me up."

Caroline whistle-snored, flapped her lips, and puffed out her cheeks, laughed till she cried when I imitated her. "Show me again how I do it," she'd say, so I'd stretch myself flat out on my back on the sofa and close my eyes and whistle and flap and puff. My grandmother would laugh, tears pouring down her face, her eyes bright and dancey. "Lord, you got a talent," she'd say and then she'd gather me up in her dry, crepey arms and kiss my face all over.

June told me Nate snored, but I never heard him do like she said, make the little chatter from his nose like the roll of a toy drum. I asked him once if he'd do it for me. He said, "Do *what*?" and I said make the little drum sleep sound. He said, "I don't know what you're talking about, and if that's something your mama told you about me, you better know there's not a word of truth to it because I have never snored in my sleep. Or awake either."

Because my father's snoring was a secret, it was even more intriguing, and I sometimes stood at the door to my parents' bedroom and listened, but to no avail. So there was all that from my past and all the new romance piled into the guard I kept the next Sunday morning, standing just outside Ada's bedroom door. After a while, I heard something that sounded like rocks tumbling under moving water, something muffled and dull and not at all what I was expecting. Maybe I wasn't close enough. I touched the knob to see if it was latched. The door gave and opened a few inches. I pressed my ear, my face, and then my whole head into that opening and my skin tingled as if I'd just passed from one world into another. The blinds were closed, so I couldn't quite see them, but now I could hear them much better. Tumbling rocks, moving water, no, it was like somebody humming a single note. One of them smacked their lips and turned, I thought for certain it was High Pockets because the bed sighed and I said to myself, *So would I.*

How loud is a sigh? I didn't hear June coming up behind me. She grabbed me and pulled me out into the hall and pushed the door to. "That's one you never learned from me," she said. "You and him and her too? Son of a bitch, Lily, you got some life ahead of you." She went into our bedroom and closed and locked the door behind her, left me standing there in the hall feeling half a fool and half a tramp, came out a couple of minutes later fully dressed and stormed out of the house.

When High Pockets opened the door of Ada's bedroom, I was sitting on the floor, leaning against the wall at the top of the stairs and entertaining myself with pictures of my mother roasting in hell—now that I had other people I could count on, I didn't so much fear her anymore, I just despised her. "What's all the ruckus?" he said, rubbing his eyes, shuffling barefoot to the bathroom.

"I heard every word," Ada called from her bed, and I followed her call to her room, the light there soft, her hair every which way. "Do you know, 'The pot calls the kettle black?' That's your mother, pot if ever I saw one." She made a place for me on the bed beside her, the sheets were still warm from where she'd lain.

I pulled the covers up to my chin. "Never mind her," I said.

"You got to mind her," Ada said. "Until you can mind yourself, that is."

"Seems to me what you need is some schoolin'." High Pockets, toothpaste white in the corners of his mouth, pajama top way too short, his fat belly showing. "School, that's the place for your mind."

Downstairs in the kitchen: waffles, syrup, fried eggs, scrapple, Ada dressed to kill in an old bathrobe of High Pockets', me just as fetching in one not quite so old. High Pockets still in his pajamas and slippers and a wool muffler around his neck. "Just don't believe everything they teach you in history class, you hear?"

I hadn't been to school since we'd left Vero Beach and the idea of it scared me because I didn't want to find out I was a grade behind, but if school was what Ada and High Pockets wanted, I knew I'd have to give it some serious thought. And of course it was *just* what they wanted, they talked about it like the very idea was a stroke of genius and they wouldn't let it alone, not that day or the next or right through the week. In fact, High Pockets even called me from Tupelo to say the more he thought about it, the surer he was that school was where I belonged and when he got home Friday night, he said he had it worked out perfect, on his way back to Mississippi that Monday morning he'd drop me off.

"Drop her off where?" June wanted to know. We were all sitting at the bar and they were tasting Kingman Brown's holiday punch, which High Pockets said wasn't as good as last year's and Ada said was better and June said was good enough for her either way and asked for another glass.

"She had enough punch till later," Ada said to Kingman Brown.

"School," I said, low-key, no big deal, that was the way I tried to sound, because I didn't want her to mess around with what Ada and High Pockets were doing with me and my new life.

"What school?" June asked, licking the rim of her glass.

"Corner of Broad and Ninth," High Pockets said. "I already dropped by, I got the form right here, need you to sign it somewhere . . ."

"Why school?" June asked, but she took the pen and scanned the form and found the line and signed.

"Why not?" Ada said.

Actually, come Monday, June was pretty nice about it. Sometime over the weekend she'd gotten to the store and before I left our room that morning she gave me a zippered pencil bag filled with some already sharpened pencils, a ballpoint pen, and a six-inch plastic ruler, and when I was dressed and ready to leave she wished me luck.

Downstairs, High Pockets was anxious about me being on time, he wanted to leave right away, even though it was only a quarter past seven. And of course it was way too early when we got there so he took me out for breakfast to the same steak-and-eggs place where we'd eaten that first morning, only we had flapjacks and sausage, not a bite of which I could digest, because he was flirting like crazy with a girl sitting by herself at a little table in the corner.

"Miss Constance, I heard you got yourself a new sweetheart. Did you tell him how you're already promised to me?" Miss Constance lowered her eyes and tugged at the handkerchief in her lap. "You tell him, you hear? I don't mind you amusing yourself for the time being, but you know my day is coming."

The boy came to clear our dishes and pour some more coffee and hot water for my tea and Miss Constance paid her bill and left without even turning to wave good-bye. "You think I embarrassed her?" High Pockets asked me. "Maybe sometimes I get carried away with myself."

"Are you and her friends?" I asked.

"Not like you and me is friends," he said.

"How are we friends?" I asked, tugging at my skirt, wishing I had a handkerchief, wondering if us being friends meant we were enemies too.

"Up close, from the day-in-day-out of it," he said. He offered me Chiclets from a package he pulled from the pocket of his trousers. "Seen the crusty sleep in each other's eyes. Share a bathroom. Hear each other crying behind a closed door."

"I heard you snoring," I said. "I never heard you crying."

"Not yet, you didn't."

I meant to look away as I gulped down the last of my tea, but something wouldn't let me, so when I spoke my eyes were still searching his above the rim of my cup. "What makes you cry?"

"Feeling happy and feeling sad, same as you," he said, and he nodded his head and cupped my chin in his hand, and something hot as it was cold descended from that place just below my mouth through every inch of my body right down to my toes. What was it about that man that moved me so? If I'd had to tell you back then, I don't know what I'd have said. I knew it wasn't that I had a thing for fat men or snaky hair. But I don't think I could have put it as simply as it was, how I loved his loving ways and the promise of his steady gaze.

I don't remember the ride to the school. I don't remember saying thank you for breakfast and the lift, or telling High Pockets to have a good week. A girl standing on the broad steps of the schoolhouse, wearing a shiny chrome badge-studded white strap across her chest pointed at the Cadillac and asked me was he my chauffeur. "What's a chauffeur?" I asked.

"Your driver, works for your daddy."

I watched the big car pulling away from the curb and then I said, "He *is* my daddy."

When I got home from school that afternoon with a black eye, June fussed over me. I didn't want to but I *still* longed to feel her care for me, so I let her. She held a towel packed with ice to my cheek and cooed, she did, that is, until I told her how I got the shiner. Then she threw the towel and the ice cubes across the kitchen. "God damn your ass, Lily Wolscy," she hollered, "serves you fucking right."

"What serves her right?" Ada asked as she struggled to let herself in the back door with a couple of full grocery bags in her arms.

"Go ahead, tell her, Lily," June said. "You think she'll kiss your feet, hell, kiss your ass, don't you?" She spat as though my face were closer to hers than it was and her saliva landed about a quarter inch from the toe of Ada's shoe.

"Ugly, what makes you so ugly?" Ada barked like a big bulldog at my mother. Then she turned to look at me for the answer, saw the color, black and purple around my eye, the rest of my face a steamy rose color from sweat and every emotion in the world.

"I got into a fight at school," I said.

"Nigger fight," June explained, "no offense intended. Told some girl High Pockets was her daddy."

Ada set the groceries down, stroked the throbbing bruise with her thumb, touched my hair like it was bruised too.

"God love a ninny," she said. "I do." She fixed another towel with ice cubes, wet the towel to make the cold come through, held it to my cheek, clucked to herself, something I couldn't make out.

"I'm not a ninny," I said.

She looked at me, matched my fierce glower with one of her own. "Like hell you're not," she said.

That night Ada told High Pockets what happened and he drove up the next afternoon, so he was waiting for me when I got home from school—seventh grade, utter embarrassment, all that time wasted—and that's when he read me the riot act, waved his hands in my face and shrieked like a woman, pulled at his hair, swore to shame June and me both, and finished with the bad news: He would love me till the day I died.

I knew June was upstairs listening—I could feel her judgment on me just as sure as if she was in the room with us. Now she hollered to me to bring her a Coke, "With a lot of ice," she called from the hall, and I didn't have to do it, I knew that by then, but now there was something in it for me.

She was sitting in a chair by the window doing her fingernails, the smell of the polish sickly sweet the way it mixed with the smell of her cigarette burning in an ashtray full of butts. The nail-polish brush shook in her hand as she cackled, "Aren't you something! You've got the love of a spook, fat and greasy, got his spook girlfriend eating out of the palm of your hand."

I did exactly what I'd gone up there to do, I emptied the Coke over her head. She cackled some more as she dabbed at her wet face with her skirt, and she didn't raise her hand to me, didn't even fake a move like she might.

"Yes, ma'am," she said, licking her wet fingers, "I guess you've got it all."

I looked at her and all I said was, "I've got more than I had."

# Chapter 17

And then I lost it, at least that's how it felt. The truth is I lost most of it, and what was left of it I had to give up, I had to walk away and leave it behind.

Except I didn't walk. I drove. In a car June got from a white man named Simon. I never knew his last name or how they met, but he had a 1952 Dodge Coronet and sometimes he'd just show up, toot the horn and call to her at the bedroom window late on a Monday or a Tuesday afternoon and June would take the night or at least a few hours off. They'd go someplace, she never said where they went or if he was rich, and I didn't ask.

But then Simon got arrested for passing bad checks—talk about unsavory business associations—and June posted his bail. I guess the checks he passed were small and so was the bond and a couple of days later, he called her from St. Louis, said he'd pay her back for the bail he'd jumped just as soon as he could, but in the meantime she could have his car if she didn't mind the leaky roof and the door jammed shut on the passenger side.

June had a fit about the money—small a sum as it was, it still set her back dollars and days, the two being equal, Memphis the place where they came together. Well, I was pissed off too, because it was the money, not a beat-up old Dodge, that was going to get her out of town. But then, as things turned out, the car was my own deliverance.

At first it was just for the hell of it. June let me drive it when she wanted something but she didn't feel like going out—a roast-beef sandwich, cream rinse, seamless hose—and I'd take my time, pick up Ada at the beauty parlor, run her over to her sister's for an hour. But soon the car gave me other things, mostly the solace of retreat from what was going on at school, more fistfights, only half of which I started and the other half I didn't know how they began, but no matter who started them I was always ready to finish them, as though I ever could, as though there was an end to the things we fought over, what you saw on the outside, prejudice and intolerance, and all the other things those two concealed, loyalty, fear.

Finally, I got suspended for ten days—the principal said he had enough to worry about with real negroes, he didn't need a made-up one adding to his problems—and it seemed like getting suspended was the thing that turned High Pockets and Ada against me, at least that's how it looked to me. What else could I make of it when he called me a jackass, only a jackass would make things harder for herself than they already were, because what did I think, that saying I was colored was going to make my life anything but miserable? And even saying I liked colored wasn't a whole lot better. "Go on," he said, "get on over to white folks' trouble, leave us colored to our own."

"What about how you said it was all the same?" I yelled at him. We were in the kitchen, he was sprawled in a chair eating a plate of hush puppies, I was standing against the back door, leaning hard on the knob so the pain it caused would make me mean as him.

He reached for the saltshaker. "What the hell you talking about, girl?" he asked.

"That first night where we went for barbecue, what you said about the rest rooms, June said using a colored rest room was all the same to me, Ada said it was all the same to her too, and you said that was just the way it was, all of us the same."

"Huh-uh," he said, pouring more ketchup on his plate. "Huh-uh, I didn't ever say that. Said that's the way it ought to be, but it ain't. And it ain't ever gonna be that way, neither. I know it all my life. Time you know it too."

He wouldn't laugh at my jokes, he wouldn't buy me a comic book or listen with me to Billy Graham's radio broadcast on Sunday mornings. I was in agony and I asked myself what could I do? Came the answer: flirt with him. So I did, and I pulled out all the stops. I painted my nails and I wore the dress June bought me for my birthday and I sidled up to him sexy as I knew how. I even sidled up to Andrew when he dropped by one night with his brother and he kept his arm around my waist where I put it and he squeezed me and nuzzled his nose in my neck and High Pockets, watching all the while, laughed in my face and called me white girl, white piece, white trash. This made me think shamefully about my past, made me wonder how much Ada had told him, and I wished my life with June had killed me already so I wouldn't have to feel High Pockets doing it now—he wouldn't even say my name or ask me how I was feeling if I answered the phone when he called from Tupelo or downtown, he'd just tell me to get Ada.

And Ada was just as bad. "What you doing home from school?" she whined a couple of mornings into the suspension. When I told her she screwed her face up at me and made little black holes of her eyes. "Look at that," she whooped. "I do believe you're a bigger ninny than I thought you was," and when High Pockets told her the rest, she laughed just like he had and said how I was wasting my time and blazing a trail directly to hell both, but she wished she'd seen it just the same, me coming on to her boyfriend, of all people, and Andrew too, because ever since her television broke she'd been missing the comedy shows, and here there was a hilarious program right in her own house, live, and she'd missed it. Then she put a stale roll in her pocket and went out, stayed away all that day and did the same for days after.

Suddenly the time I had on my hands was pure torment. All the hours I had to dwell on how they'd deserted me were like a noose around my neck and my own self-pity just drew the rope tighter. In my mind they became the two most detestable people in all of creation, maybe there was still hope for me and my mother. Sure.

"Don't come moping around me with that sorry puss," June would say when I'd go upstairs to our room in search of comfort, looking for it in a bureau drawer or in the closet, since it was clear I wouldn't get any from her. "What the hell do you want, anyway?" she'd ask, but I didn't know, or I knew but I couldn't say, because when you are fourteen, you don't think to say, "I want something to take away this awful goddamned feeling." So I'd grab up an old magazine from a pile on the floor like it was just what I'd come for, or I'd light one of her cigarettes and smoke it hard and fast right down to the filter.

She wasn't always so callous. "You're going to make yourself sick smoking like that," she said one afternoon. It was a few days after the long Thanksgiving weekend. I'd gone back to school, where nobody talked to me except to call me the same old names only now I didn't want to start anything, so

I left right after the last class and ran most of the way home. It was half-past three. The light outside was pale, the weather had been overcast for days, the sun never more than a white blur low in the sky, no lamp turned on in the bedroom, the smoke from my cigarette and all of June's still hanging thick in the air. She came up beside me and held out a package of spearmint gum. "I know you won't like hearing it from me, Lily, but Ada and High Pockets, they're doing you one big son-of-a-bitch favor."

I took a piece of gum and tried to make her out in the scant light. It frightened me that she'd noticed the change between me and them, it made it more real. I pushed my tongue against the raw place inside my cheek where a bully's punch had landed the day before, and I worried a tooth that wasn't loose and then I put the gum in my pocket and left her there.

Downstairs at the bar, Kingman Brown poured each of us a tall glass of Kool-Aid. "Where Ada at?" he asked me, as he added a shot of bourbon to his glass and stirred it with his finger.

It seemed like everybody wanted to talk about the same damned thing. "How am I supposed to know where Ada is?" I snapped at him.

"Supposed to know because the two of you been stuck to each other like paper to glue ever since you come here."

"Well, it looks like she got herself unstuck," I said, a little less snappy. "High Pockets too."

Kingman nodded and turned on the tap behind the bar and began to wash the sinkful of glasses. I studied a catalog from a bar-supply company in Knoxville—jiggers, swizzle sticks, garnish trays. He looked up at me, scratched his chin with the back of a sudsy hand. "They watching out for you, child," he said. "And it's a good thing too, since everybody see how you decided not to do it for yourself."

He was standing beneath one of the new brass lamps that hung from the ceiling, and in its glow his light-brown skin was a warm yellow-gold, and his kinky hair was a circle of tight little lacy curls. "What do you know about it?" I asked him, with less bite to my voice than there was to my words.

"I know what everybody around this joint know, how Ada and High Pockets loved you, how you loved them back like they was your family, but they wasn't, and they can't be. Too bad. Clear to me what pass for love in your family don't hardly pass at all. Still, it count for something that your mama know enough to agree with the rest of us, even said it to me direct: she making money off this deal, you making a serious predicament. At least there's some sense in her, a lot more than you're likely to find cozying up to that Andrew."

I went back upstairs. June was listening to Arthur Godfrey on the radio. Like I was in a trance I took a couple of dollars and the car keys from her pocketbook. She started to ask where was I going, but all she got out was the first word. "Where?" she said, and I said, "What?" but I think we both knew we weren't either one of us going to finish our sentences.

It was fully dark by the time I pulled away from the curb in front of the house. I drove around the neighborhood for a while, wishing I had some errand to run for Ada or June, someplace I had to go—much as me and June had traveled thousands of needless, senseless miles, still I wasn't in the habit of driving *myself* nowhere. I got lost a couple of times, but then I realized that it really didn't matter where I ended up, so I tried to relax and make a game of it, and by the time I got hungry I was on the other side of town headed east. That's where I read the sign that said it was forty-four miles to Bolivar and for the moment I thought maybe that was the perfect thing to do, to take a ride over and visit with the man who'd sold Ada his dishes and glasses. But then forty-four miles sounded too far to go to find a man whose name I didn't know, and I had nothing else to go on either, no home address or place of business, no heart.

I pulled in at a White Tower instead and I had one of their omelettes, all puffed up like they made them, and a stack of white toast with strawberry jam. Then I paid my bill with some of the money I'd taken from June, dropped a dime in the round tin with the picture of the crippled girl, walked out the door and threw up in the parking lot, sat cold and clammy in the car with the radio on and the heater turned way up, praying to God to not let me have polio and get me back to Antonia's alive.

Which He did, but that's all He did. I mean, nobody greeted me like I was the prodigal child. In fact it seemed like they hadn't even noticed I'd been gone. I walked through the downstairs rooms, watched June deal a hand of cards to a couple of men I'd seen around, saw Ada talking to the new cook in the kitchen, and neither one of them so much as nodded in my direction. Andrew was there but I rushed past him and I didn't turn when he called me Honey Pot and asked me could he have a taste. I was halfway up the stairs when I heard somebody crossing the barroom floor in a hurry. I thought it was Andrew, so I made to move faster but then I heard the man call my name and it was Kingman Brown. Was I okay? His skin looked just as warm in the dull light of the hallway as it had looked that afternoon by lamplight. Did I need anything? Did I ever. But I didn't say so.

It took me a few months, right through the winter, before I could keep down a White Castle omelette or drive farther than the city limits, the one being somehow related to the other. June didn't notice the few dollars here and there, or if she noticed she didn't give a damn, so in addition to feeding myself, I was putting some money aside, though if you'd asked me what I was saving it for, I'd probably have said I wasn't, seemed like it was just accumulating of its own will. And maybe that's the point, that it took me a long time before I realized I was shaping my will.

What I did in the meanwhile is sometimes go to school, but mostly I didn't. I kept the Dodge tanked up on the cheapest gasoline in town, I plugged up the hole in the roof with a rag from the cellar and long strips of black electrical tape, and drove aimlessly, trying to find some ease in the fact that I had nowhere to go and nothing and no one to go home to, except for Kingman Brown, who made it his job to ask after me—How was I doing in school? What did I get for Christmas? Would I be his Valentine? I'd answer him with the truth, or I'd make up answers, or else I wouldn't answer him at all, but I liked having what I could feel behind his questions—somebody keeping an eye on me—and sometimes it felt like it was the only thing that kept me from disappearing altogether.

The holidays passed—there was all kinds of doings at Antonia's. In fact it seemed like there was parties all the time that winter, for somebody's birthday, a dead president or a regular customer, or else somebody died, or had an accident. There was parties for people just married and one for a couple just divorced—I remember thinking I didn't know colored people got divorced—the two of them there celebrating, drinking toasts to each other, June flirting with the husband, kissing the face of every card she dealt him, tickling him under his chin with the white silk flower she'd pinned to her dress, Ada and High Pockets dancing on the bar with the wife and then with me, and wasn't I surprised when they reached right down and hoisted me up there beside them so the next thing I knew we were laughing like old times, hugging one another, our feet slipping on spills, the music and the smells and the heat from their bodies shaking me right down to my bones. But then the record changed, and Ada said she had to stop and catch her breath and High Pockets saw a friend putting on his coat and off he went, off they both went and all of a sudden here's Andrew at my feet— some things are so predictable—his face shiny with sweat and his lips and his yellow eyes sloppy with liquor, and he's pull- ing and tugging at me till I all but fall from atop the bar down into his arms, the music louder now, my substantial height and weight and my voice raised in protest nothing to him, nothing to anybody else either I guess, for how he car- ried me, unimpeded, out to the kitchen and down the stairs to the basement.

"What the hell you got there?" How I blessed the sound of that voice, Kingman Brown's, and he was loaded down with a half-dozen bottles from the cellar storeroom, but he dropped them, all six of them, and they broke on the cellar floor as he reached both his hands to take me from Andrew. "I didn't know you handled freight, I'm going to keep you in mind come inventory time."

He shooed Andrew up the steps and sat me down on an old kitchen chair. "Oh my God, oh my God, oh my God," I said.

"You gonna be okay, girl, you just take your time," he breathed the words, each one like a gentle and comforting touch.

"I'm okay, I'm okay, I'm okay," I said after a bit.

"That's right, that's good," he went on, and he looked at me and I must have looked as right and good as he hoped I would because then he teased me, "Ain't no hurry except I got to get back upstairs so make it quick," and when I grinned at his teasing he asked me would I dance with him a little later, but in the meantime he wanted to get me some- thing to drink and something to eat, there was black-bean soup on the stove.

"Black bean sounds good to me," I said and we stood to

climb the stairs. But then I turned to face him because there was something I needed to straighten out. "He didn't do it because he's colored," I said.

"No," Kingman Brown agreed, and he waited a second, long enough to look at the spilled liquor on the basement floor and back to me. "No, but he might have done it because you're white," and then we stood there long enough for both of us to get inside what we'd just said like a coat we didn't either one of us want to wear but it was the only coat there was and it was too cold to go without one.

Upstairs in the kitchen he filled a cup and grabbed two spoons and he had me stand behind the bar with him and share the one serving, his eyes popping from his head as he watched June, sitting at a table across the room and letting Mr. Oliver put her hand deep into the open fly of his trousers and then tuck a tip into the top of her stocking, Kingman Brown's tawny cheeks blushing like he'd never seen anything so scandalous—I suspect the scandal wasn't so much what June had done as it was my seeing it—and I blushed too for all the other things I'd seen, never mind the things I'd done, Andrew's move no more than a piece of my past catching up with me, a close call I couldn't blame on June.

"What you looking at?" Kingman Brown half scolded me. "Don't you have school tomorrow? You better get yourself upstairs and into that bed," and he gave me a little shove and I went.

Not to sleep. Just to wait. Until I was sure I couldn't sleep—and I hardly ever did. Then I pulled on my jacket and slipped out the door, ran through the freezing rain to the Dodge, sat with the motor running until it threw off some heat. I drove to some place along the harbor and watched the boats sitting quiet in the river. After a while I cried and missed my mother in the backseat, wrapped my arms around myself like there was two of us, me in need and another to care for me, and then I rubbed my sex, softly, gently, crying softly still and on and on.

Through the winter months, I never really left Memphis, but early that spring I'd sometimes cross the bridge and head into Arkansas on U.S. Route 70 until I got tired or hungry or just plain sick to my stomach from being in another state, like intestinal gas was a geographical matter. Then I'd turn around and drive back to the White Tower where the waitresses and the cooks all knew me. They brought me cups of hot tea and one of them, Sue, brought me Easter cookies she'd baked at home. Her skin was as gray as her hair and her eyes and she smoked cigarettes—Salems—and drank black coffee like smoking and drinking was her job. But she was kind to me in the silent way kindness is sometimes most appreciated, ran out the door after me if I dropped something from my wallet, stood in the parking lot and buttoned up my jacket.

That winter had seemed endless until it was gone and then I had no memory of it, the ash trees frothy with white blossoms, the chinkapin flowers soon browned and curling, the sky scrubbed clean. And now I tried stretching the distance I'd go in the Dodge. I even went looking for High Pockets once down in Tupelo, crisscrossing first the city streets and then the back-country roads, looking to spot the Cadillac, and seeing more than ever of what I'd seen before.

In Tennessee I'd been the object of it, but the Mississippi version was somehow more malicious, with its signs of racial hatred and promises of violence—those horrid words painted on homemade billboards and even posted right in the middle of people's front lawns. Once when I stopped for something to drink I watched an old colored woman leave the store with a five-pound bag of rice pressed tight to her side, walking so bent over she couldn't keep her head up high enough to see where to step or how to fend off the stones white boys threw at her from the window of a passing car. I felt afraid and ashamed for how I couldn't stop it, but I didn't try. Then I wondered if High Pockets would say I'd done right or wrong. On the way home I wondered if Lucas ever did anything like the boys in the car and I decided he certainly never had and I thanked God for his kindness, felt sad and sorry for how unkind I'd been to him.

The next day was my fifteenth birthday. June gave me a card and an IOU for a present, came home a week later with a white angora sweater, hot and itchy, and too tight for me by a mile. I wore it anyway and Kingman Brown noticed it, asked me was it new. "I got it for my birthday," I said.

"When you had a birthday and didn't tell me?" he asked in that voice he had, like he was angry with me but I knew he wasn't.

"Last week," I said.

"Shit," he said.

He came to work late the next day. Ada gave him hell and he gave me a necklace, a single cultured pearl on a gold chain. "You can tell it's not real gold," June said to him, as she fingered it where it was already hanging around my neck.

"That's right, but it's a real pearl," he said.

"You wait and I'll get you the chain," June said. "Mr. Oliver's taking me downtown tomorrow, I'll have it for you tomorrow night. You wear that cheap thing, it'll turn your neck green. I'll get Jess to buy you something good, fourteen karat, maybe you can come with us, he says he wants you and him to be friends, he says he has some people he wants you to meet, his kind of people, Kingman knows what I mean, don't you, boy?"

"I don't want a fancy chain," I said, "I want this one. And don't call him 'boy.' He's got a name, it's Kingman Brown, as if you didn't know it."

"Oh, Lily." June tittered. "Why don't you give it the hell up?"

I wanted to say something smart, but this one question of hers was bouncing around inside my head, asking itself again and again till my brain was fevered with it.

Kingman Brown clucked, "Um, um, um," and Ada called June from the kitchen, said she wanted to talk to her about some business and I got in the car and drove directly to the White Tower looking for Sue. She wasn't there. The cook said she'd had to leave for an emergency, her husband was hurt and he'd been taken to the hospital and she'd rushed there to be with him. I got somebody to write down the name of the hospital and how to get there while I drank some iced tea and I pressed the pearl into the hollow at the base of my throat, making believe it was a charm meant to protect me and Kingman Brown and Sue and her husband.

She was sitting in the emergency room picking lint from the sleeve of her sweater. I called her name and she looked up. "Great sakes," she said. She had big dark circles under her eyes.

"How's he doing?" I asked.

"He's doing okay," she said. "Cut his leg bad, lost a lot of blood. They're stitching him up now. But listen here, come sit down beside me and tell me how you got here."

"I drove," I said, as though that was what she wanted to know.

"Well, I know you drove. I mean what are you doing here? What made you come?" She pushed my hair back from my face, tucked it behind my ears. Then she hugged my cheek with her dry hands like I was the one whose life was in peril.

Some people were hollering across the room and I looked around to see what the commotion was for. It was a colored couple, and the woman was giving the man hell about something. That's when I realized everybody sitting in the emergency room and the doctors and the nurses too were all colored. Sue saw it on my face. "He's colored, my husband is," she said.

"I have some colored friends, I mean they're more than friends really, I live with them, me and my mother, but we're not friends anymore, it's not working out, none of it is, and I went to the White Tower because of the cookies I guess and the cigarettes and they said you were here so I came to tell you good-bye because I'm leaving town tonight which I didn't even know until this very instant, just right this second as I'm speaking to you is when I figured it out."

Sue had dropped her hands from my face and she was looking at the place at the base of my throat where the pearl lay. Now she pulled at her bottom lip with her fingers, first just away from her teeth, then up and over her top lip, like she'd sealed something inside her mouth.

"Mrs. Grayson," a nurse said crossing the room to stand beside our chairs. "You can see your husband now if you'll come with me."

Sue got up from her chair and bent to kiss my forehead. "I see you got yourself a pearl," she said as she gave me a book of matches and a couple of cigarettes from the pack she had in the pocket of her uniform. "Do you know how real pearls get made?" I shook my head no. She brushed her hands across her face as though her own touch could make things right, which in some way it could, and then she pulled her bottom lip away from her teeth and unsealed the words. "Sand. Sand gets inside a oyster shell and makes a little sore and then the sore grows and grows until it becomes this beautiful seed. That's what you are, you were born of somebody's soreness, you were a bother inside them, but you grew into a beautiful lustrous girl."

★

Some people save the best for the last, hold it all back and then just when you need it most, they let it rip. Like Sue. Like Kingman Brown.

I called Antonia's on the emergency room pay phone, hoped he'd answer. He did. "Evening," he said.

"Hi, it's me, Lily."

"Where you at?"

"It doesn't matter. I'm just calling to say good-bye."

"Where you going?"

"That doesn't matter either. Except when I get somewhere, can I call you up and you'll send me some of my things? Well, my clothes is all I got. Come to think of it, forget it."

"I ain't going to forget nothing," he said, and then he whistled like men do at a pretty woman, but he didn't mean pretty. "What am I gonna do with you gone? What am I gonna do not knowing what's happening to you and are you okay and did you find somebody to take care of you? How am I ever going to find a girl I can care for like I care for you, tell me that?"

"I got the pearl you gave me," I said, quiet so nobody else could hear me. Not that anybody was listening. Huh. I know what it was. It was the first time I ever made love on the telephone, first time I ever made love to one person who stood for everybody else I ever loved, and it felt holy, the way it does when you're in love, inside of it. I touched the pearl, it was like touching myself, not my sex, my soul. "I'm wearing it right now," I said, "and I'm not ever going to take it off."

"You call me soon, you hear," he said, and I could tell the lovemaking was over for how his voice had changed and I stopped touching the pearl and I swallowed hard like I had love in my mouth but now I had to eat something else. Over the telephone, I could hear a man's voice, maybe halfway across the barroom at first, then coming closer to Kingman Brown, and then the voice of a woman, it was June, I couldn't make out what she was saying, but I knew the sound of her laughter. "Thank you for calling," Kingman Brown said, all business now. "Good luck to you out there, you hear?"

It was so damned hard to hang up, as though once I did I couldn't call him again, or change my mind, thinking maybe I could leave in the morning, or hell, leave next week, or wait until after the Fourth of July party they were planning, maybe I'd stay on and graduate from junior high school, another two years, make some friends, sure, and clean out the spare room for myself. Jesus Christ.

I hung up and the dime dropped into the coin box. I pulled another dime from my pocket but then I looked at it like I didn't know what it was. " 'Scuse me." A pretty negro lady with her hand wrapped in gauze was waiting to use the phone. I put the dime in my pocket, went back to where I'd been sitting with Sue and smoked one of the cigarettes she'd given me, picked at my cuticles, and watched the lady talk on the telephone. When she finished another lady made a call, it must have been long distance because she dialed "0" and then she put in a lot of change. She talked for a while, and then the phone was free again, but a boy about my age jumped up from his seat at the other end of the room and made it to the phone in a big hurry like he'd been waiting and I left.

I drove the Dodge into the filling station across the street from the hospital and I told the colored man who came to the window to fill up the tank. He asked me did I want him to check the oil and the radiator and the tire pressure— looked like rain to him, did I need new windshield-wiper blades because they were running a special? I told him to give me the works and went inside and bought a package of cigarettes, Salems, and some Chiclets from vending machines, lit a cigarette, peeled the wrapper off the gum and popped a couple pieces into my mouth. The man came inside and said I was all set and I paid him for the gas and the rest.

"You setting off for somewhere?" he asked me. "How far you going?"

I turned the gum over in my mouth. "Why do you want to know?"

"Well," he said, eyeing the roll of bills in my hand, "I don't usually like to give advice when it isn't asked for, but I got to tell you, you'd do best to hide your money somewhere."

Now I looked at what I'd saved—it was mostly singles, but there was some tens and twenties in there too, all told it was close to $200—and I smiled as I stuffed the money into my shoe.

"Thatta girl," he said. "Say, you need any maps? I got Tennessee and Mississippi and this one of the southeastern United States. Here," he said and he gathered up one from every slot of the wire rack on the counter, "why don't you take one of each. You never know."

You never know. On the other hand sometimes you do.

I knew my name. I knew my face in the mirror. I knew there was no place more a home to me than any other and if that made me fearful it also made me brave. I had some idea of what love was and what it wasn't, and though surely I'd made some grave errors in this department, by the time I left Memphis I was beginning to understand that people who are not your kin can love you good as those that are, and often better, and that love for a day is a pleasure but love for a lifetime is only a dream. How sex and love went together was still a mystery to me, but I didn't doubt that they were real, I mean they weren't nothing, everything was something, sex and love and race and spirit too, June was something, Ada and High Pockets were something, as a matter of fact I myself was something.

So was the colored man traveling with his son, they were both named Warren and headed for Alabama and I picked them up outside of Statesboro, Georgia, about a week after I left Memphis—the maps the man at the filling station had given me were still folded on the seat beside me. Tampa and Vero Beach and Covington were all pulling on me, especially Covington, and Caroline and maybe even Nate. But that pull wasn't strong enough, or else there was another one stronger, so when I'd gone nearly as far east as the continent permitted, I turned right around, a colored man and a boy for company, and I headed west.

The Warrens were trying to get home to Birmingham and I said what the hell, I'd take them there. It took us about twelve hours and we drove straight through. We sang all the way, gospel songs mostly, which I learned fast and the son Warren said I was as good as his sister. I asked him what his sister's name was and he said Lucille and I thought about asking him did he know the truck stop in Demopolis but I didn't bother.

The father Warren said there was a lot of trouble in Birmingham, and he asked me did I want to help them make some more. What kind of trouble? I asked him. Integration, he said. I looked at him and I looked at the boy and then I said I'd take them there but I probably wouldn't stay, I'd already made enough of that kind of trouble for a while and I had some things to figure out. I was hoping he wouldn't ask me what kind of things I had on my mind, since hate was certainly one of them, so was evil, and Birmingham was a damned good place to get some firsthand experience of the two of them, but it wasn't experience I needed, it was understanding. I went through all that in my head like I had to defend myself, and then he just said where exactly was I headed because he didn't expect as much of me as I did of myself. I said Albuquerque, and this time I knew I wasn't lying, it was my Nashville and this was the journey I had to take to find out who I was and something wasn't the whole answer.

It was after midnight when I left them off downtown. I pulled into a rest stop on Route 5 just outside the city and I slept deep and dreamless until the morning, and then I started making my way and when I saw a sign later that day that said it was 211 miles north to Memphis—I must have been somewhere around Jackson, Mississippi—I hesitated for a second and then I put my foot on the gas and floored it and by the next day I'd crossed Louisiana.

I was a few miles east of the Texas border when I saw a roughly hand-lettered sign, CHENILLE BEDSPREADS FOR SALE, and I stopped to look, because even though I didn't have a bed, I had a picture of myself living in Albuquerque: a little adobe house, a cactus garden, a dog, maybe a German shepherd, and a chenille spread. A half dozen of them were hanging from a clothesline stretched between two trees, mostly they were all one pastel color, one was a red, white, and blue rebel flag. But they were cheap, you could see right through them, and the patterns were thinly tufted.

The lady who was selling the spreads also sold sandwiches and cold drinks from a cooler in the backseat of her station wagon. I bought ham and cheese on a roll with a grape soda, and sat on the back fender of the Dodge to eat and drink my lunch. I was thinking about buying another sandwich when I heard a telephone ring. It was the strangest thing out there in the middle of nowhere. I looked around and there was the booth on the other side of a picnic table, which I hadn't noticed either. The bedspread-and-sandwich lady answered the phone like she'd been expecting a call, as if it was her own personal line. She talked for a long time, waved to a couple of people who tooted their horns at her as they drove by, left the phone hanging from the cord to go look at something in the glove compartment of her station wagon, went back to the phone and talked some more, laughed, raised her voice in disbelief. She hung up the phone when a man in a panel truck pulled up beside the Dodge and hollered, "Let me have a couple of cream cheese and olive sandwiches, Louise, and make it quick."

I pulled out the change from my pocket, counted it, it was near to four dollars, and I had to wonder if I'd been saving it up for just such an opportunity. I finished the last of my grape pop, and tossed the empty in a box of them Louise had beside her wagon. Then I asked her if she minded if I used the phone and she winked at me.

The operator took her time answering. I gave her the number at Ada's and she told me the first three minutes cost $1.70 and I dropped in the money. June answered on the first ring, though her "hello?" was more a question than a greeting. I said hi, it was me and she said God, Lily, and I realized she'd probably been right there by that telephone ever since I'd left.

I heard her strike a match and take a drag from a cigarette. Then she said it was a lousy connection and I said I could hear her okay and she said it hardly mattered since she didn't know what to say and I said I didn't either. "But don't hang up yet," she said, and I said, "I won't."

"Where are you calling from?"

"Outside of Shreveport."

"So far away?"

"Seems close to me."

"Christ, Lily," she said, and I said, "I know," and then we were quiet for a while again and I liked it that way, the sound of her breath and mine, and now I could hear other things too, the water running behind the bar, Louise and the man laughing, cars passing by, June taking a big drag of her cigarette and then exhaling. Finally one of us said, "Miss you so bad," and the other one said, "Me too," and then we hung up.

## ABOUT THE AUTHOR

Susan Thames is a member of the creative writing faculties of Sarah Lawrence College and Columbia University, a member of the editorial board of Global City Press and a contributing editor to *Global City Review*. She is the author of *As Much As I Know* and co-editor of *The Breast: An Anthology*. Her home is in Brooklyn but her heart is in Manhattan with her godson, Evan.